ARCH-DIVINITY

SOUL RIVER

MILTON & HUGO L.L.C.
4407 Park Ave., Suite 5
Union City, NJ 07087, USA

Website: *www. miltonandhugo.com*
Hotline: *1- 888-778-0033*
Email: *info@miltonandhugo.com*

Ordering Information:
Quantity sales. Special discounts are granted to corporations, associations, and other organizations. For more information on these discounts, please reach out to the publisher using the contact information provided above.

Library of Congress Control Number: 2024911146
ISBN-13:   979-8-89285-085-8   [Paperback Edition]
                   979-8-89285-086-5   [Hardback Edition]
                   979-8-89285-084-1   [Digital Edition]

Rev. date: 05/23/2024

CONTENTS

CHAPTER 1

ARCTARA

(Year 254 of the Tribunal Calendar, Month of the Virgo)

The golden embrace of the sun bathes Athens in a luminous cascade, casting a spell of brilliance upon the ancient city. Its rays danced on every corner, igniting the vibrant pulse of this bustling metropolis. From the majestic marble columns of age-old temples to the kaleidoscope of tourists and locals weaving through its streets, Athens is ablaze with the promise of joy and prosperity. In this sun-kissed haven, hope and optimism are woven into the very fabric of its being.

A steady stream of farmers, laborers, and elites bustled through the labyrinthine roads, hustling to and fro amidst the ceaseless tide of people.

Crowded roads reverberated with the rhythmic clatter of hooves and the lively hum of chatter and conversation, as the eclectic populace carried out their daily affairs.

Engaged in trading goods, managing civic affairs, or simply savoring the sights and sounds of the bustling marketplace, the throng seamlessly interwoven within the crowd's ebb and flow, each individual a crucial thread in the vibrant tapestry of the community.

Many temples, each hosting its own enclave of clergymen and divine relics, adorned the cityscape. From the majestic tower dedicated to the city's patron gods to the more obscure altars honoring minor deities, these sacred structures provided a window into the rich and diverse beliefs of the people.

The air hummed with the melodies of hymns and prayers, as devout worshipers knelt before the statues of the divine beings, offering their praises and tributes.

The flicker of candlelight danced off the ornately carved figures, illuminating the intricate details of their features and robes, evoking a sense of majesty and awe.

Amidst the bustling spectacle of civilian life, almost as if orchestrated, the powerful presence of the Athenian Guards cast a formidable shadow as they strode confidently through the streets, their bronzed armor gleaming in the sunlight.

Around the necks of each guard, they wore bronze necklaces which showed their ranks, their honor over their fellow guards.

The formidable warriors moved with an air of discipline and precision, a testament to their rigorous training and skill.

The metallic clink of their weapons and armor seemed to softly hum through the city as they maintained a watchful eye on their surroundings, ever vigilant to any potential threat.

Their imposing presence served as a reminder of the strength and sovereignty of the Athenian state, instilling a sense of safety and security among the populace.

The common belief was that prosperous times produced weak men, but the strength of the Athenian army made such ideas fall apart.

Atop the towering walls of the city stood the foremost defenders of Athens: the fabled Guardians. These elite sentinels were the cream of the crop, their names were spoken with reverence and deserved admiration throughout the lands. Not only did they secure this era of peace and prosperity through centuries of sacrifice, but they now protect and maintain it, much like a lioness watching over her cubs.

Clad in sturdy armor and steeped in battle-hardened experience, they maintained a vigilant watch over the city. From their elevated vantage point, they surveyed the farthest reaches of the horizon, ever alert for any looming dangers or threats that might encroach upon their beloved Athens.

In the annals of history, these formidable warriors stood as the epitome of Athens' indomitable spirit. Their courage was a beacon of inspiration, casting a shadow of awe upon their enemies and showing reverence to their allies. Their intimidating prowess was not simply a result of their arms, but a testament to the unwavering resolve of a united people defending their cherished city-state. In their presence, the air itself seemed to crackle with the tension of an impending conflict, serving as an unmistakable warning to anyone who dared to test the mettle of Athens.

Shrouded within the depths of a tranquil, softly illuminated alley, Archeus fixed his steadfast gaze upon the lively throngs of Greeks traversing the nearby streets. For countless cycles of the sun and moon, he had dedicated himself to the pursuit of understanding the intricate tapestry of this metropolis, meticulously studying and deciphering the rhythms and rituals of its inhabitants.

His sharp eye and impeccable memory allowed him to meticulously document a vast array of particulars — from the intricacies of attire to the nuances of dialects and the unspoken rules of social norms — details that might slip by unnoticed to the casual onlooker.

Archeus understood that to seamlessly integrate into this unfamiliar realm, he must grasp its intricacies fully. Thus, he lingered in the shadows, a discreet yet vigilant observer, biding his time until the opportune moment to traverse these streets without restraint.

It's remarkable how much one can learn from the shadows. To the eager eyes of tourists chasing fulfillment, Athens was the epitome of euphoria, the pinnacle of human aspirations, the ultimate destination. But for Archeus, a wanderer from distant lands stranded in unfamiliar territory, there lay much more beneath the surface – particularly, the timeless expressions etched upon the faces of the locals.

Archeus observed everything, from the condescending attitudes of undeserving nobles to the despair that enveloped the children of the city's underbelly. With each passing day, he came to a singular realization: the labyrinth of marvels that would later fill the pages of tourist guides was likely nothing but a veneer. Indeed, the true measure of a city's prosperity lies not solely in its grandeur, but in the contentment of its common folk.

Despite the striking parallels to his former world, Archeus sensed the wisdom in his decision to operate from the shadows. In a land rife with unspoken socio-political disparities, who could predict the plight of an unwelcomed outsider?

ARCHEUS

Upon awakening in this unfamiliar realm, I discovered a new identity adorning me: Archeus, a name that instantly captivated the imagination of the locals. The details of my arrival—the how, when, and where—presented themselves as enigmatic puzzles, yet memories of my origins remained readily accessible with each passing thought. My journey began in the barren soils of Earth, in the distant year of 5187 GD, a time and place not known by the inhabitants of this realm.

Alas, my entry into this world coincided with its impending demise, amidst the twilight years of the Third World War, heralding the dawn of the epoch known as "The Great Decline." From the moment of my birth, I witnessed the unraveling of civilization, a poignant reminder of humanity's inexorable march towards its own undoing.

Before the onset of the Third World War catastrophe, numerous predictions were suggesting that no clear winners would emerge. It was believed that the aftermath would regress society to medieval times, dominated by petty conflicts resolved with rudimentary tools like sticks and stones. History proved them partly right.

In the aftermath of the war, essentials once taken for granted—electricity, cars, and medicine vanished—plunging the world into pandemonium. However, the Third World War didn't unfold with the anticipated nuclear weapons, but rather with biological weapons that spread deadly diseases, drought, widespread famine, and other extinction-level events.

My time on Earth wasn't marked with status, fame, or dreams of luxury. Amidst the tumult of a planetary conflict, like those around me, my mindset boiled down to one imperative: Survive. Yet, the threat of biological warfare loomed large, and soon I found myself succumbing to a terminal illness that ravaged my immune system.

It wasn't uncommon to find me unconscious for days, engaged in a relentless battle as my body and cells fought fiercely to endure.

After succumbing to the relentless onslaught of this man-made illness, I eventually drew my last breath, having known nothing but the horrors of war. And, as many religious fanatics had prophesied, there appeared to be life after death indeed. I cannot say how long my breath had forsaken me, but when my eyes fluttered open once more, I found myself in an unfamiliar realm — the heavily guarded precincts of Athens, the domain of nobility.

The mystery of my arrival baffled not just me, but anyone capable of understanding. My sudden appearance ignited chaos and swift apprehension. Events unfurled with alarming speed, and before I could comprehend the gravity of the situation, I was already marked for execution.

The rapid pace of events left me bewildered. How could I have known that commoners weren't welcome there? And it's not as though I was there by choice... or was I?

I pondered whether my detainment was due to my dark skin and curly hair. It seemed plausible, as I stood out amidst a sea of fair-skinned individuals with diverse hair and eye colors—an archetype reminiscent of the fantasy worlds depicted in virtual reality games.

In hindsight, it was understandable, considering the Greeks had never encountered individuals with my melanin before. From their perspective, they might have perceived me as a demon from Tartarus or, at best, a rare anomaly that somehow survived to adulthood. Regardless, the conclusion was clear—I needed to be purged.

Back on Earth, I had witnessed humanity's exploitation driven by primitive ideologies surrounding race, gender, nationality, religion, and more. It was disheartening to encounter the same antiquated mindset in this new world. It had taken centuries of protests and critical analysis for humanity to acknowledge that racism hindered progress. Yet, even then, in some corners of the world, it persisted, albeit more subtly.

How long would it take for these nobles to grasp the same understanding? I didn't hope for long, as my life hung in the balance.

As with most societies, this world — Arctara — also had a caste system. In Greece, there were slaves, commoners, warriors, nobles, and royals. These are the primary classes within the caste system.

The primary classes had slaves who endured terrible treatment. No one would care about their lives, and coming from a modern world, I couldn't help but feel helpless while witnessing the barbaric mindset the ancients possessed. However, it was wrong to judge them by comparing their methods with modern, more developed standards. A world that revolves around war and survival has no concerns for humanity and ethics.

Commoners are individuals who receive legal protection under the laws of the Greek's city-states. They form the backbone of Greece and have the right to possess property and own land within its boundaries.

Despite these privileges, many choose to reside outside the cities in villages, as they deemed cities incompatible with a simpler way of life. Moreover, city life proved to be very uncomfortable for most commoners, so unless required, civilians preferred to distance themselves from such places.

This indirectly proves to be one of the sources of control for the Oligarchs and rulers.

Warriors are individuals who volunteer to fight during periods of war and eventually become so proficient at it that they pass down their knowledge and experience within their families, creating an occupation of blood.

Given their commitment, warriors earn respect and fear from all societal classes— even nobles and royals place them in high regard. In times of war, between the nobles and the enemy are the shields and swords of warriors and the fortified city walls. Unless necessary, making an enemy out of warriors is the last thing anyone would do.

Unlike the nobles, warriors were more simple and united. Attacking a warrior who has not committed a taboo was like attacking the entire occupation, which is not something any city-state dared to do.

Similar to knights on Earth, warriors occupied a status between that of a noble and a commoner. They held the right to land ownership, traditionally passed down through the male lineage of a family.

That being the case, there were not many warriors in Greece, with their numbers barely being around 10,000. With such a small number, there was no need for much consideration from those in power.

Although the number was not high, it made up a great part of the overall population of Greece. After all, Greece is an ancient kingdom with barely 300,000 to her name.

Nobles are individuals who are said to be able to trace their lineage back to mythological figures, but there is no concrete evidence to support these claims. Under the status of nobility, they are entitled to privileges that know no bounds. Their primary fear, however, remains the royals.

Not every city has royals, but those that have them stay quite distant. The amount of power they held was not something some city-state could dare ignore or threaten.

Royals were not different from monarchs in the territories they governed. They held court and ruled, with nobles under them. To show how unique royals were in this ancient world, the place they ruled was very similar to a small kingdom, with Royal Knights and strict codes of law.

In addition to the aforementioned classes, there existed other classes, such as merchants, doctors, and priests, who did not fall into specific places in the established caste system. However, it is generally agreed upon that individuals who are able to improve or bring benefit to a city-state, hold the same class as warriors or even some nobles.

Merchants, who engaged in trade and commerce, enjoyed the profits that came with it; doctors used their skills in medicine to treat various ailments, and priests played a critical role in tending to the spiritual needs of their community.

As I found myself in a cell, shock overtook my body, leading me to question if it was due to the presence of unknown diseases or something else.

Coming from modern times to an ancient world, I knew it could be a challenge to endure a multitude of diseases since my immune system would require significant adaptation to confront and overcome them all. There might be diseases in this world that Earth has never experienced before. Whatever it was, I was in deep trouble. I have always had a high susceptibility to illness, even a mild case of the flu could leave me incapacitated for a few days.

With an unknown sensation traveling through my body, I pass out. However, amidst my descent into darkness, I could hear the guards shouting as if grappling with a challenging situation.

The only thing I heard before darkness consumed me was the gentle voice of an elderly woman speaking in an unknown language, and for some reason I could vaguely understand the meaning of, "Take... this... I will.........take...him... with me."

PART 2: MOTHER

After who knows how long I slept, I woke up, only to find my surroundings unfamiliar once again. The good thing was that it was not the cell, which I had expected to see... it was different.

As I tried to get up, I realized I was strapped to a wooden platform, with the faint aroma of medicinal herbs entering my nose.

Straining my neck to look around, I saw there was a container full of foul smelling liquids, which had a darkish color and a pungent smell, at the feet of the platform. The smell was familiar, and it didn't take long for me to realize what it was.

Blood!

Hiss!

A faint pain on my wrists caught my attention, causing a sudden sense of fear to overcome me. It did not take a genius to guess what happened. After I passed out in the cell, someone moved me and did a bloodletting ritual on me... Which means the liquid in the container is most likely my blood!

It was unknown if this person was friendly or not. Only doctors from medieval times and witch doctors conducted bloodletting.

Looking around, there did not seem to be any strange symbols, which meant it was possibly a doctor.

I couldn't help but sigh in relief; at least it wasn't a witch doctor. If it was, my organs would have been harvested, with my skull cracked open, in order to 'cure' me. However, why did I not feel light headed or sick? The illness that was bothering me seemed to have disappeared. Instead of weakness, I felt a never-ending stream of power flowing through me, making me feel quite strong. I felt I could kill a lion in a single blow.

However....

Looking at the amount of blood in the container, I was confused.

If a human lost a lot of blood, surviving alone would be a miracle, let alone waking up. In the container, there was at least 3 - 4 gallons of blood, making me question if humans ever had that much blood.

With confusion in my mind, I laid there. There was nothing else I could do anyway. Hoping that I would not be going back to that cell, my mind drifted, and I was lost in thought.

From the little of the world I saw, it was clear this was not Earth, at least the one I was familiar with. There were no clouds of darkness or acid rain. The earth was not barren and could yield crops.

I have never seen the sun before, nor smelt a refreshing wind in my life. This world was definitely not Earth.

The Third World War started when I was 3 years old, so there's much of Earth I had never gotten the opportunity to see. If not for technological advances, such as virtual reality and the Second Earth, I probably would have ended up being even more barbaric than these people.

As the hours etched on, my thoughts were the only companions in this unfamiliar place. I did not mind reflecting on the life I lived. There were not many fond memories to cling to, but it was all I knew. Perhaps if someone from an earlier time were to be placed in my situation, they would be worried and anxious to return home however, I did not have those thoughts. I did not have anyone on Earth to miss or to be missed by.

Earth was a lawless land, with survival of the fittest being the mainstream. It was killed or would be killed. I never understood the urge to want to live on in a world with no prospects or care for human lives.

I crawled over corpses to prolong existence, but at what cost? I lost my humanity and grew cold to the world. Perhaps I was no longer human; the only thing I could be was a demon!

My hands were stained with the blood of others, but aren't they the same? At least I had the decency to create a burial site for those I consumed...

Eating humans. Truly, I had fallen so deeply that I could no longer see the light. Even if the light once again shines on Earth, it will not shine on me. Darkness was where I belonged.

Sigh.

As my thoughts were taking over my mind and the faces of the ones I'd killed flashed through my mind, the distant footsteps of someone faintly reached my ears.

Creak...

The sound of a door opening echoed out, making my body tense up faintly with nervousness and fear.

With the door behind me and footsteps drawing near, I couldn't see who walked in.

It didn't take long for the person to appear before my eyes, examining me with medicine in hand. The person exclaimed slightly in relief upon seeing I was awake, causing me to lower my guard. It didn't look like they were dangerous or had ill intentions towards me.

The person was an old woman with a warm and gentle disposition.

At the time, I didn't know this woman would become my mother in this world.

Despite her advanced age, Maria carried herself like a young woman and moved with grace. She possessed an inviting and gentle aura that I found surprising. I had never seen someone like her before, but that was no surprise because a ruined world brings the worst out of people.

Her hair, which used to be golden blond, now withered from age. Her blue eyes seemed to contain the ocean, as when you'd look at them, the illusion of ocean waves could be seen.

After living with Maria for close to three years, I could not help but be curious about her origins. This entire time, she had not disclosed where she came from, but I could tell she was not from Greece. Call it a gut feeling or whatever, but it was evident that a pride superior even to that of the Athenian people resided within her. She was like oil to water in relation to the Greek people. From afar, they would look similar, but with closer observation, the difference would become evident.

From her medical skills alone, Maria's knowledge was not something anyone from this world should possess, yet she could turn ordinary herbs into life-saving medicine. If that were all, it would have been remarkable, and could be considered a genius, but she was also proficient in weaving, cooking, literature, foreign customs, and possessed many other skills.

What she went through to develop these skills was unknown, but even if I had the opportunity, it would have been unlikely for me to achieve the same.

In my first year of being in Maria's company, I tried to communicate with her, but as I had expected, there was a language barrier between us. However, after bringing some items and having me name them, she started speaking to me in broken English, which made me feel both shocked and numb.

I had never heard of something like this before, but Maria was far greater than a mere genius. It would normally take years for someone to learn a language, but she only needed a few seconds?!

No one could be this terrifying. If Athens knew such a monster existed within their land, how would they react? She absorbs everything she sees, which becomes nutrients for her growth. Military tactics, language, geography, etc.

If they knew, it was very possible I would no longer look like a demon to them, as a true demon existed next to me.

Though worrying, I was happy to witness this scene. I could finally communicate with her and learn more about this place.

From Maria, I learned a lot about this world, which was called 'Arctara' by the Greeks and Romans. Pronouncing the word was quite strange, as it seemed to not belong to Greek or Latin but some other ancient language.

I also came to realize that Arctara could be divided into three domains: the Western Plains, the Northern Highlands, and the Eastern Boundaries, to understand the world. It helped a lot that the world, although different from Earth, still shared roughly the same geography.

The Western Plains represented the landmass that comprised the Americas of Earth and its various islands. Within this domain, one could expect to find an array of Native Indian tribes and many other indigenous people that have thrived in this region for thousands of years.

Contrary to the physical traits commonly associated with the Native Indian tribes, Maria's appearance bore a striking resemblance to that of European nobility. Her refined and elegant features, combined with her graceful demeanor, showed a stark contrast to the rugged and earthy characteristics typically linked with the Native Indians.

Maybe she wasn't from Greece, but what about Rome? It was a possibility.

The Northern Highlands were diverse, encompassing several civilizations that have played pivotal roles in shaping the history of Arctara.

This realm included ancient empires such as Rome, Greece, Persia, and Egypt, along with many other fascinating civilizations. The relationships in this area were deep and complicated. For example, Greece and Rome used to be one entity, but differences emerged once Rome began to capture territory and welcome foreigners into it.

The Greek people did not like change and did not see eye to eye with those they saw as lower-class people. To them, the land was created for them by the gods; they would not share it.

Egypt was even more complicated. It was both a friend and an enemy to Rome. Friends because of their trade and enemies because of distrust.

Egypt felt Rome's ambition was too strong, and it was scary as they had the might to back it up. After thinking, they came up with a strategy to survive for as long as they could. As soon as Rome moved towards them, they allied with Greece and fought against Rome. However, this balance was very unstable and could collapse at any time.

The Eastern Boundary is a treasure trove of ancient wisdom, comprising many great empires, of which India and China are a part of. Maria did not know much about this region, as they tend to remain in isolation, causing the region to be filled with mystery.

There were records of people arriving in the Northern Highlands from the Eastern Boundary to conduct trade, but that was many years ago, so it is hard to say if it's true or not.

I was once again amazed by the knowledge that Maria possessed. Even the Greeks and Romans, who were well known on Earth for their wisdom, did not know much about their world apart from their surroundings.

Then again, it was rare to find anyone exploring the world with all the factions and wars that broke out randomly. Traveling was a testament to seeking death!

The Northern Highlands were divided by many forces, with Greece located on the southern edge of the landmass and the Persians bearing down across the sea. Rome was located in the middle of the continent, with its back to the northern sea. To their right was a vast piece of land occupied by many scattered but united forces. On their left was a vast land of trees and mountains, home to the Barbarians.

From all of this information, I was able to discern that Arctara is vastly different from Earth. There were some similarities, but there were far more differences. This world is likely a parallel world.

On Earth, some historians have suggested that there may have been around 1500 city-states that existed at the same time in ancient Greece. In Arctara, however, the number of city-states was much smaller, with only fifty existing. This difference might be small, but if one were to think about the world at large, how much have these historical differences affected the world?

Although I was unsure of the cause, I couldn't shake the feeling that there might be a hidden history that could shed light on the reason for this divergence. Perhaps buried beneath the countless layers of time and obscured by the veil of forgetfulness, there existed a narrative that could unravel the mysteries of the past and provide crucial insights into the present. It was this sense of curiosity and wonder that drove me to pursue a deeper understanding of Arctara and to uncover the secrets that lay just out of reach.

Regardless of location in the Northern Highlands, it seemed that recorded history only extends back a few centuries, leaving me to ponder what events took place and what factors might have caused them. Nevertheless, even in the absence of a well-documented historical narrative, one could still piece together fragments of the past through artifacts, folklore, and other clues, providing a closer idea of the past.

Among the fifty city-states that existed in Greece, three in particular shone brighter than the rest: Athens, Sparta, and Corinth.

Although all the city-states in this world had some religious affiliation or tradition, not all of them were said to be founded by deities. Others were formed by the geographical location itself.

The exact role that religion played in the founding and governance of each city-state varied, and as a result, some were positive and some were negative. Nonetheless, none of the city-states escaped the influence of religious belief in the gods. The degree might have differed, but the presence of the gods was clear in the lives of the people.

In the Northern Highlands, the ancient people possessed a remarkable set of skills and abilities, particularly in the realm of warfare. Despite their impressive capabilities, there was a pervasive sense of reverence and caution towards the gods, making one speculate that their potential may have been suppressed out of deference to divine power.

I have heard of this before. Back on Earth, before the spreading of science and knowledge, humanity was held hostage by the Church. Anything the Church did not want people to know was branded witchcraft, causing many brilliant people to die and the era to stagnate.

Many people have said that if the Church had not done so, the world would have progressed far faster. But I was not sure if the Third World War would still happen or not as a result.

PART 3: TRIBUNAL

In matters of worship across the city-states, a powerful collective known as the 'Tribunal' held sway. Comprising a diverse group of priests and priestesses drawn from all the major temples, the Tribunal wielded formidable influence in determining the will of the gods and communicating it to the people.

Whether it was Greece or Rome, none of them dared to oppose this force. No one knew who was actually a member, making things even more frightening – no one wanted to make an enemy; they couldn't fight.

Throughout history, those powerful men who reach a level of status that many would envy, after turning their faces at the temples and the gods, all of them mysteriously vanish.

Even a demigod, a warrior revered throughout the Northern Highlands, someone who could be said to rival the gods, could not escape the fate of 'disappearing'.

Sparta was known for its deep reverence for the God of War, Ares, as well as other deities associated with martial prowess, such as Athena. Nevertheless, it was Ares who occupied the central role in Sparta's religious life. For these fierce warriors, devotion to Ares and emulating this god represented the path towards becoming a powerful warrior.

Strength was what the Spartans admired above everything else. If they died, that only meant they were weak. This trend of thought seems to be woven into the core of Sparta.

According to legend, Sparta is home to the descendants of the legendary Spartan warriors, whose valiant defense at Thermopylae has showcased the masculine power of strong warriors. Even when faced with thousands of enemies and despite their deaths, these legendary

Spartans carved out a path of blood, leaving the enemy frightened and hesitant to invade Greece.

Today, the descendants of these legendary figures underwent even harsher training, pushing their bodies to the limit, hoping to follow in the footsteps of their ancestors.

Even if they were far from what their ancestors could do, they were not something just any warrior dared to face.

A single Spartan warrior is said to be worth 10 times that of any other warrior. These are not baseless words but proven by combat, time and time again.

Even in times of conflict in Greece, Sparta remained peaceful. Their reputation could be seen in this. Because of how powerful they were, more and more people started to believe the legends and stayed a wide distance from them.

Legend has it that the Spartans were imbued with a potent combination of divine bloodlines, drawing on the strength and courage of two of the most revered figures in Greek mythology: Heracles, the mighty demigod renowned for his valiant deeds, and Ares, the God of War known for his ferocity and martial prowess.

Despite their assertion of divine lineage, those who would claim to be the descendants of the gods seemed no different from any other mortal beings, apart from their level of combat capabilities.

Corinth, a city renowned for its royal class, possessed a strong monarchy that set it apart from the other city-states. In this society, the king was held in the highest esteem, and the temples of the gods owed their existence to his benevolence. His influence was felt throughout the city, with his commands being obeyed without question and his voice carrying the weight of the law. Indeed, it was said that a single word from the king could lead to the death of anyone who dared to defy him, leaving no exceptions or clemency offered. Such was the power of kingship in Corinth, a city where law and hierarchy were elevated above all other values. Yet, this system had its own strengths and weaknesses, and the conflicts and struggles of those within it were complex, shaped by the competing forces of tradition, ambition, and human emotion.

Observing the world from my perspective, I could see that Greek mythology differed in many aspects from its portrayal of Earth.

On Earth, Zeus was often portrayed as a promiscuous being with an insatiable sexual appetite, engaging in relations with various creatures, including his own offsprings. This resulted in the creation of numerous demigods and true gods. However, in this world, Zeus was depicted as a fair and wise ruler, seeking to improve the world through just and lawful means. He held all the gods accountable for their actions and readily punished any wrongdoing, even stripping them of their divine status.

On Earth, the gods were often imagined as titans, towering over all with control over the forces of nature.

In Arctara, the gods were depicted as spiritual entities who could only be seen if they chose to reveal themselves. They existed in a form that was beyond human comprehension but could be accessed through faith and devotion.

Not only that, but due to the obscure nature of history, the stories of many minor gods and heroes seemed to have been excluded. There's a possibility they never existed, and I was more inclined to believe that.

The difference between 50 and 1500 city-states was not a small thing. Many figures would not have even had a chance to be born, let alone the gods they believed in. Also, among the gods that were traditionally worshiped, there were new gods added that didn't exist in the myths of the Earth.

Of course, this could have been an oversight on my part. The mythology of Greece was so vast that it is very likely I did not remember it correctly. After all, I learned most of these things from virtual reality.

Despite my prior assertions, I couldn't observe any evidence of divine beings in this world. The locals here would attribute any phenomenon they weren't able to explain to divine intervention. Conversely, when they'd comprehend something, they'd attribute their understanding to divine guidance. This phenomenon wasn't exclusive to this world; the inhabitants of Earth, as well, have always tended to attribute 'miracles' to coincidental occurrences.

To confirm the absence of divine beings, I embarked on a journey across various city-states, cross-referencing their respective mythologies and histories. Through this, I discovered more inconsistencies than concrete evidence, solidifying my belief that gods did not exist.

As an outsider, I was uncertain of how these gods might perceive me, prompting me to exercise caution in my actions.

Ironically, maybe because I absorbed something on the way from Earth to Arctara, I gained three abilities that made me no different from a god: Eternal Vigor, Time and Space Control, and Over Element.

If someone owned even one of these abilities, they would be worshiped by the ignorant ancients, yet I possess three. However, the way I discovered them made me question if it was actually worth it.

When I gained enough confidence to explore the world, I started my journey. I made sure to wear a cloak to keep my identity a secret. However, there was one thing I did not count on: I was not used to the ways of life in the Northern Highlands, where carriages were the norm and many people would travel by them.

While walking on the street, despite being aware of a noise that was getting closer to me, I didn't associate it with a carriage, and before I could even react, I lost my life. Everything happened suddenly, so I was not prepared. Oddly enough, even when I was dead, I still felt alive.

There was pain, but I still lived. While confused, I only helplessly closed my eyes as my eyelids became heavier and heavier with dizziness as time went on.

Upon awakening, I discover myself buried in a coffin, only to die of asphyxia. This repeated over and over again, until I was able to pry the coffin open and climb my way out of the still-loose dirt.

If someone was at the scene, they might have suffered a heart attack seeing a demon crawl its way out of the depths of Tartarus.

To be honest, though I did attain immortality, the overwhelming memory of death left me with a deep sense of fear. The state between life and death was frightening. It was akin to a frozen wasteland, where nothingness was the norm. There was no light, no deity, no paradise, just an endless void.

Eternal Vigor might not have been a gift, but rather a curse that could lead to eternal agony. Although it wasn't clear, it is very possible that Eternal Vigor also grants eternal life, but depending on how you look at it, it is still a curse.

Imagine the scenario where Arctara gets destroyed. I would then be the only one left to drift in the cold embrace of space, never to taste the sweetness of death.

Based on my various experiments over the years, it appeared as if Eternal Vigor allowed me to regenerate lost limbs. Furthermore, any detached body parts seemed to vanish upon the completion of the regeneration process.

If I had been on Earth before the Third World War, this would have been a godly ability to have. Unfortunately, I still doubt I would have lasted long under the biochemical weapons, even as an immortal being.

Although this power was good, so was science. When science reaches the extreme, it is no different from magic.

There was one unsettling aspect of Eternal Vigor that left me shrouded in skepticism: would I be able to revive myself from nothingness — without any physical remnants? I was apprehensive about putting this thought to the test and being proven wrong, so instead, I would assume that complete annihilation would spell my demise. Even though a part of me could sense vaguely that I was truly beyond death.

It was an uncanny feeling. It was similar to how one knew they had to pee without checking their bladder.

Despite the passage of the years, my physical form remained unchanged, devoid of any tell-tale signs of aging. In fact, my appearance remains the same as the day I first arrived in this world, apart from three changes: my hair, eyes, and body.

My wooly hair has become straighter and filled with power. If someone were to use a knife to cut my hair, sparks would fly, but the hair would remain untouched. It was a very strange change. It was still normal hair, but at the same time, it had become far more than that.

When it came to my eyes, the brown color I once had took on a yellow hue, which was not much different from gold.

As for my body? It had been reforged by unknown means. My once overweight body had become chiseled like marble and turned into a statue. I surpassed the beauty standards for males and touched into the realm of the divine.

This change happened after I was able to withstand the diseases of this world, or maybe I got rid of whatever I was carrying. If this change had happened when I came into this world, I doubt Maria would have been able to cut my wrist or find any wounds to heal.

According to my test, my physical capabilities had been elevated to a level beyond mortal comprehension. I could leap a height of ten meters, shatter a boulder the size of a human with minimal effort, and move at persistently high speeds without ever feeling exhausted. All aspects of my body had been imbued with divine enchantment, bringing me closer to the realm of the gods.

It is hard to find an aspect of myself that pales in when faced with a god.

Even the simplest of my bodily activities produced effects beyond the parameters of what most could fathom. A single deep breath within the confines of a small room could rapidly deplete the oxygen inside, while exhaling had the potential to create a miniature tornado.

Merely being in my presence would instill a profound feeling of oppression in humans, similar to the sense of helplessness one experiences when confronted with a ferocious apex predator.

My physical appearance was striking and unparalleled; my straight, jet-black hair cascaded down my chiseled, statuesque face, further accentuating my deep golden eyes. Standing at an impressive height of 6 feet, my toned physique boasted an impressive set of six-pack abs that illuminated with an inexplicable bronze radiance, further amplifying my otherworldly aura.

PART 4: DIVINE ABILITIES AND TIAMAT

It wasn't until I secretly departed from Athens that I stumbled upon the extraordinary abilities endowed to me by Time and Space Control.

The dangers associated with traveling between city-states were severe and sometimes even fatal, with the penalty of death being a reasonable and not uncommon repercussion. Unapproved travel was prohibited, as it carried the potential for igniting conflicts between the various city-states.

The prohibition of unauthorized city-state travel was due to the many grave risks such actions could pose, including the theft of crucial intel, gaining insights into the political and military power structure, fomenting civil unrest, etc.

I was traveling secretly, not even telling Maria about what I was doing. I did not want to alarm her or draw attention. I expected this journey to take weeks, but while traveling by horseback, with each step, the horse and I arrived a couple of meters ahead.

It was not difficult to link this with me since I already had Eternal Vigor at this time. After a few attempts, I was able to reproduce the effect of, which was undoubtedly, Teleportation!

The further I delved into this otherworldly skill, the more bewildered and astounded I became.

This was not teleportation but something even deeper. I was controlling space itself. This ability seemed to reach a stage of controlling time as well. My power had no limits, and I soon realized it when these two abilities joined and became one, 'Time and Space Control'.

With Time and Space Control at my disposal, I could effortlessly teleport myself to any location within my line of sight. However, as I continued to hone these formidable abilities, I unearthed an awe-inspiring power — the capacity to craft dimensions, turning me into a deity-like figure with dominion over my self-fashioned domains.

Through Time and Space Control, I possess the ability to command time, including the capacity to travel back to the past — to my point of origin in Arctara and progress forward into the future, but that would cost a lot of divine power.

I decided to call the power that fueled my abilities "divine power."

My last divine ability, Over Element, gave me the power to control the five elements of creation: Fire, Water, Wind, Earth, and Metal. By combining these elements, I was able to create hybrid elements like Ice, Thunder, and Light.

I also discovered this ability during my journey towards the surrounding city-states. Once, I found myself caught in a storm, lost, and unable to find my way. Without any expectations, I simply made a wish for the storm to vanish. And it did.

However, this action exhausted my reserve of divine power, and I blacked out.

Upon regaining consciousness, I realized that I had been asleep for a couple of hours, judging by the horse that was still by my side and the still wet ground.

It didn't take me long to realize I was controlling the elements that created the physical world.

Similar to when a dragon gets older, my divine power has reached a stage surpassing my wildest imagination, leaving me to ponder the unbridled extent of my strength.

I could sense that by exerting the entirety of my powers, I could effortlessly demolish Athens without feeling the slightest hint of depletion in divine power. Of course, I would never sacrifice the lives of more than 120,000 people just so I could test my strength.

With my divine powers continuously strengthening, it wouldn't have been far-fetched to deem me a divine entity.

With the standards of power within Greek mythology, if I was to estimate my current strength, I would be considered a demigod, merely one step away from achieving true godhood.

Godhood...

Even if I had the power to rival a god, at the end of the day, I wasn't one. However, since my ambitions and plans included gods, I decided to create my own power system, founded upon the principles of Greek mythology, with certain aspects derived from my own personal ideas and inferences.

Human - normal people with no exceptional qualities about themselves. Most people in Arctara fall into this level.

Exceed - people who can do things normal people find unbelievable. A good example of this is Olympic-level athletes.

Gifted - people who can access and master supernatural power. They are generally able to live a really long time without being affected by otherworldly power.

Ancient - these are beings that are capable of ruling over a region. An example would be a Giant Dragon who grows stronger the longer they live.

Demigod - beings that are able to fight against those with divine power while not being true gods. These beings are born of divine and mortal heritage.

True God - beings that rule over a particular domain, such as love, war, death, and more.

Primordial - predates the formation of the universe and is thus not bound by its restrictive rules. They can shape the world as they see fit and achieve true immortality because they embody a concept themselves.

I recognize that individuals with absolute power, such as myself, might be inclined to seek world dominance. Although I had contemplated similar thoughts, I harbor no desire to wreak havoc on the world. However, it is undeniable that my actions will cause havoc.

To prevent such catastrophic outcomes, I created Tiamat as a means of channeling my immense powers and keeping them in check.

Tiamat was a world that would become the world of gods in the future.

As the creator of Tiamat, I would be able to create any function rules I wish. Just like the five elements can create the universe and set rules, I could do the same.

Anyone who reaches the level of demigod under the sphere of control of Tiamat must ascend, or they will be obliterated by the power I sealed inside it. This rule was essential if I wanted to create a functional fantasy world. While freedom wasn't a priority for me, it was a factor that had to be considered and restricted.

Tiamat is a dimensional world that existed independently of Arctata. Hence, if Arctata were to be destroyed, Tiamat would still exist, as the reason for its existence relies solely on me.

Tiamat's size was directly proportional to the strength of my divine power. As my divine power grows, so will any world that I create.

At the moment, Tiamat can be compared in size to Athens, with no sign of slowing its growth. The land in Tiamat was exceptionally durable, far surpassing that of Arctata. Even if a nuke were to go off, not much damage would be done; maybe a car-sized crater would be enough. And if there was any damage, it would recover over time.

Teleporting from the alley, I appeared in the Village of Crista, one of the three villages named after Athena's three daughters, Euterpe, Thalia, and Crista. In this world, Athena was not a maiden but a mother with children.

As I gazed at the exquisite night sky, a sensation of wonder and excitement washed over me. This world, unlike my previous one, remained untamed and uncultivated, brimming with endless possibilities for exploration. The prospect of embarking on countless adventures and forging my own path, altering the future of this world, struck me with immense anticipation.

I will not permit this world to succumb to despair, as my previous one did. And for that to not happen, it was imperative that I regulate the pace of technological advancements, yet, at the same time, that meant I had to discover another viable alternative to science that could fill its void.

Creating a fantasy world would be intriguing since it would shift people's focus toward surviving and flourishing with the aid of magic and the pursuit of vanquishing mythical creatures like dragons. It would divert their attention from science, meaning the world of destruction I live through would never appear here.

Had I not possessed these divine abilities, I'm not sure if my ambitions would have sprouted. The image of Earth still lingered fresh in my mind, driving me to desire control over the direction of this world. Possessing the power already, it only made sense for me to utilize it.

Arriving in front of a familiar old house, I stood there for a while. Emptying my mind of all distractions, I pushed open the front door and stepped inside. "Mother, I'm back," I said warmly to Maria, who was cooking in the kitchen.

However, before I could even fully set foot in the door, she began hurling angry words at me. Despite her harsh retorts, I couldn't help but relish the fact that I had someone to worry about.

I had never experienced this feeling before, not until I finally found someone who cared about me. Until I found my Maria. At first, it was scary; I feared that it could become a weakness, but over time, I came to enjoy it.

If one never had something good in their life and then got to experience it for the first time, it was very unlikely for them to let go of it.

Looking at Maria, I only saw a concerned mother worrying about her child.

In my memories, I could not remember the image of my parents. Sometimes I wondered if they were alive would I be complete and not be a puzzle that needed to be put together....

The aftermath of the Third World War had left countless individuals orphaned, myself included. At the time, I was 17-year-old, which somewhat dulled the impact of this plight. Yet, regardless of one's age, a person's parents hold tremendous significance in their life.

There are so many things I never got the opportunity to experience. Perhaps I can now, all thanks to Maria.

"Archeus, where have you disappeared to? I firmly warned you against using your powers, as they are unnatural for humans to have. If someone finds out about this, it will surely trigger panic." Exclaimed Maria, glaring fiercely at me. Nevertheless, I could sense that her anger stemmed from a place of genuine concern, making me feel warm.

Maria did not need to say it out loud, but I knew the reason I would cause panic was my appearance. Honestly, I didn't know if it was because Maria was also broken like me or because of her upbringing, but I was surprised by her open-mindedness and approach to things.

Despite me looking like a demon in the eyes of the Greeks, Maria saw me as her son. I could feel this very clearly.

Frankly, I didn't mind living in the shadows since it gave me ample time to diligently work on my plans. Yet, due to Maria's cabin's proximity to other dwellings in the village, rumors began to swirl around that she was insane. They were not aware of my presence, so everyone believed she was talking to herself at home.

With the addition of my divine abilities, it became easier to hide. Even if I were to stand right in front of someone, unless I wanted them to see me, they couldn't. This was very similar to the account of the gods in this world.

Although I could suppress the noise caused by her chatter, Maria forbade me from doing so. She had made it clear that she was not fond of my divine abilities. I did not know the reason for this, but I decided to respect her wishes when she was around.

"Mother, you do not need to worry since there isn't anyone capable of harming me. Besides, I've just completed the creation of Tiamat," I reassured her before opening a hole in space, showcasing the scene of a new world.

Since Tiamat was just born, there were still many things missing, but over time, they would not be less than Arctara. It would only be better than Arctara.

Thanks to my ability to control time, there was no need to wait for too long; however, the cost of it was too much for a little demigod like me to bear.

"Is this the land of Tiamat? I presume it's time to commence with your plan," Maria said, her voice laced with apprehension and slight unease.

Judging by the way her emotions were fluctuating, she did not mind me using my powers, or maybe she did not notice.

Looking at her with a serious look on my face, I firmly said, "I intend to use this village as the core of my plans. This way, I can get further with bringing the world I want into fruition."

As I glimpsed over at Maria, I observed that her demeanor had been replaced with worry. I was able to understand the reason for her concern, but this was a matter of utmost importance to me, one which I simply couldn't surrender, not even for her.

Undeniably, my intentions may not have been entirely virtuous; however, my success would undoubtedly enrich the lives of many. No matter where one resides, death is an inevitability we all must face. Well, except me...

Cradling my hand softly, Maria spoke up, "Archeus, I still do not think it is right for you to pretend to be a god. However, I like this plan you have and will support you."

"Thank you, Maria."

Immense warmth washed over me as Maria's words reached my ears. It took a lot of effort to convince her, causing us to have plenty of arguments in the process. While I could have started my plans without her, I did not want to do that. She was the most important person in my life.

It was hard to find someone who would care about me; there was no way I would hurt or toss her aside. I planned to take her along so she could see and experience a world she never had before.

Seemingly remembering something, Maria rushed into her room and returned with a yellow leaflet in her hand. "The outcome of your blood test has arrived. August informed me that I can merge with your blood, but there is a high possibility of failure."

Maria's words delighted me as I reminisced about the time I provided August, a scientist, with a sample of my blood a year ago.

I had given August the blood sample with the hope that Maria could merge with it, attaining immortality. In times like these, surviving beyond the age of 50 was deemed an exceptional feat - even a simple malady could potentially claim one's life. Therefore, Maria's survival was ever more precarious.

I was not sure if it was because of Maria's medical expertise or if it was fate, but it was shocking for her to live to such an old age. Even though she was 61 years old, she had the energy of those much younger than her.

Though I felt gratitude towards August's assistance, there was something about his character that made me apprehensive. It was akin to being in the presence of a devious serpent, always scheming and operating covertly.

"Do you trust August?" I inquired.

I, myself, never trusted him; if not for the need to get results, I wouldn't have handed over my blood. Even though I normally had no fear of my blood falling into the wrong hands, there was something about him that caused me to feel slightly worried.

Maria shook her head and clarified, "While I cannot say that I entirely trust him, I am confident that he harbors no ill intentions towards me. August's intentions are clear and straightforward: to create an ideal race capable of evading mortality, which is why he is involved in research. However, people have branded him a demon due to his reluctance to provide his research to those in charge."

So he was basically like the scientists from Earth who, in the early days of the Church, were apprehended, branded as witches and demons, and burned at the stake.

In the end, it's knowledge. Without knowledge, the things one can do are limited.

"Are you completely certain about fusing with my blood, considering the potential side effects?" I was experiencing mixed emotions; even though I wanted her to attain longevity, I was hesitant about the risks that she might face, which could adversely affect her well-being.

What if she were to die? What would I do?! Picturing a world without her in it wasn't something I wanted to do.

That sense of loneliness that I used to feel before knowing her was frightening, even to an immortal being. Having companions on this path would make the journey bearable.

"Even if I don't take your blood, I will most likely die in a few years. So I might as well risk it and hope it succeeds." She replied, determined.

That's right, Maria was currently in her 60s; it was a miracle for her to live this long, but we had no guarantee about tomorrow.

Observing her unwavering resolve, I remained silent. Steeling myself, I clenched my teeth and teleported the two of us to Tiamat.

Appearing inside Tiamat for the first time, the two of us surveyed the surroundings, realizing we were on a lofty mountain peak, which gave us a panoramic view of a vast expanse of land.

Although I created Tiamat, I had not yet taken the opportunity to experience it, and as I wanted to surprise Maria, in a way, it was also a surprise for me. One thing that caught my attention right away was the fact that we could survive in this world, and the realization made me happy.

While it seemed like a risk to bring Maria here without knowing for sure if it was safe, I was overwhelmed with relief after finding out that she was not in danger. If one was to look around her, they would notice layers upon layers of space protecting her.

CHAPTER 2

LURKING SHADOWS

(Year 257 of the Tribunal Calendar, Month of the Scorpion)

The skies were darkened, with the pale moon sitting ominously on the horizon as if bearing down on the world. From a mortal perspective, there was nothing odd about the moon, but for those outside the realm of humanity, what they would see when they looked up at the sky was a crimson moon, which seemed to have been created fully from blood and gore.

Large parts of the world were covered in this crimson hue.

Although the crimson moon covered a large part of the world, there was one place in particular where the rays were darker and beaming down like a demonic stairway to the moon.

Below the moon, on the ground, stood a large pyramid that occupied a vast portion of land. On top of the pyramid, floating a couple of feet off the ground, was a golden carriage being pulled by two white lions with eagle wings.

The winged lions looked ferocious and noble at the same time. Within their ferocious eyes, there was a hint of divinity. It was not hard for those without knowledge to see that these were divine beasts living in a different world than normal creatures.

The carriage, at first glance, looked odd...It was not only large in size but also shaped like a temple. The carriage was adorned with many murals of kings and gods. Each side depicted a different scene, some of the divine wars and some of the mortals worshiping what seemed to be towering figures.

The carriage was more of an artifact that should have been placed in a museum than a carriage that should have been used. One could only imagine the amount of money needed to buy it. But one thing was certain: it probably was not something a nation could afford.

From this vantage point on top of the pyramid, in a single glance, one could look across the land of Egypt, witnessing its ancient wonders and endless desert.

Running violently through the land of sand was a river that stretched far and wide, making the area closest to it greener and more lush than places further away.

Atop the pyramid, only the carriage and the crimson moon seemed to exist in peaceful harmony. However, that was short-lived, as five shadows could be seen rushing towards the ancient monument.

The shadows were so fast that not even a hint of sound was heard or the sand moved. Their speed seems to transcend everything around them, as the world could not affect their movements.

It took a mere second for the five shadows to arrive next to the carriage and kneel without hesitation. No one could tell if these figures were male or female, as their figures were obscured from view under their black cloaks, with not even a hint of skin showing.

One of the figures, perhaps the leader of the group, spoke with regret and disappointment in his voice, "My Lord, we have failed you. We have searched Egypt from top to bottom, but we did not find any trace of her."

Within the carriage, a vague genderless silhouette could be seen drinking a cup of tea. The words of the shadow did not seem to affect the Lord, but the momentary pause of their hands said otherwise.

The Lord seemed to ponder for a moment: "We have searched Rome; we even created some enemies in the process. Now, we're searching Egypt, and she is still nowhere to be seen. That only leaves Greece. This might be a problem. Our relationship with those three old things, is not good, so they might interfere if we take action." The voice of the Lord was odd; it was like many people were speaking at once, some female, some male. However, despite this, there was a gentle and warm feeling when the voice reached the ear.

The five shadows remained silent, as it was not their place to advise their Lord. However, they knew how difficult it was to deal with those of Greece because of what happened in the past.

Seemingly coming to a conclusion, the silhouette of the Lord reached into their chest and took out an object with a groan before placing it into a sealed box.

With a weaker tone, the Lord spoke, "If I know the Tribunal, if you give them this, they will turn a blind eye for at most five days. So, in that time, no matter what method you use, bring her to me!"

Taking the box in hand, the leader of the shadows' face changed as he realized what was in the box: "My Lord! This…"

"No need to say anything; just bring her to me. If that item falls into the wrong hands, this sacrifice will be worthless. Do you understand me?"

"Lord! We will not disappoint you. Wait for our good news!" The shadows disappeared faster than when they arrived.

On top of the pyramid, once again, the carriage and the moon were alone.

The moon seemed oddly different; compared to before, the redness had dimmed significantly.

The Lord sighed and sipped the cup of tea, feeling downcast. "I might have made a sacrifice for no reason. I can already foresee that item not falling into my hands; what a pity. These subordinates of mine think too highly of me. I am no different from them; even I must play my role to survive."

Sensing something, the Lord sighed again, causing the lion beasts to rise into the air and break apart space before going into a bottomless hole and disappearing from Egypt.

Not long after the carriage disappeared, a red beam of light streaked across the skies, scanning the land, before landing atop the pyramid.

The figure was a tall, falcon-headed god with dark skin and mysterious runes on his body. Around his neck was a golden necklace, which seemed to be part of a ceremonial dress. He was wearing clothes unique to Pharaohs, but clearly, he wasn't one.

In his hand, he held a spear a lot taller than him that pulsed with power.

Grasping the air with his free hand, the falcon-headed god found his hand to be empty and frowned slightly in surprise. Not many could remove traces of themselves within such a short span of time, and definitely not from him who ruled the skies!

Pondering for a moment, his eyes glowed with divinity, and he peered in a direction. Before leaning backwards and throwing the spear with such power and speed, the air seemed to explode, and the earth trembled!

Wherever the spear reached, space shattered as if it were made of glass. The spear moved on its own, changing direction as if it had a will of its own.

BOOM!

Within the space, a collision echoed, with cracks appearing in the skies of Egypt. The moon and stars in the skies swayed as if they were about to fall!

The falcon-headed god grasped him once again, and he could feel something struggling to escape him. He could see that if he continued, he would not succeed. He was not on his home turf, and the distance between him and the enemy was too vast.

He could only release his power and feel as though the enemy had escaped.

The spear, as if it had received a command, broke through space and returned to the falcon-headed god's hand.

Looking at the tip of this spear, which was dented slightly, astonishment and curiosity appeared in his mind. Not many people could damage his spear; who was that person?

It did not seem to be a god, so maybe a demigod?

"Interesting; things are becoming quite interesting, no?" The falcon-headed god shook his head with a smile and disappeared in a flash of red light.

Cloudy skies were obstructing the view of the packed cityscape below. The city was dark with lamps and lit torches, casting shadows that extended in all directions.

Few people could be seen walking through the streets on their way back home from a long day of work.

All the merchant shops and carriages were nowhere to be seen. Everything was the same as usual, but to some, the air hung with ominous premonitions.

On the balcony of the Royal Palace, an old man wearing white royal garbs stood imposingly, looking out at the streets and the city as a whole, with wisdom in his brown eyes. No one knew what he was thinking, but his unmoving posture and cold glare in his eyes could cause a person to shiver.

The old man had been standing there since early in the morning. He had not moved, seemingly lost in thought.

Behind the old man, a female's impatient voice rang in the silent room: "You called me here, but you have not said anything. What could be so interesting out there?"

Both of them had things to tend to, but here they were, wasting time as documents piled up.

"There is always something to be seen when one actually takes the time to look for it. Reading reports can only paint a picture of what is seen from the perspective of the person who wrote them. My father said those words to me before, but I have never understood them until now."

The old man sighed. If not for an incident that caught his attention, maybe this would have continued, and maybe Corinth would have ceased under his rule. If that happened, he wouldn't dare think about meeting his forefathers in the afterlife.

"Irene, tell me. What do you think about the current situation of Corinth?"

Irene, who was sitting at the war table, was confused and did not understand why he asked this. Corinth is currently a prosperous city-state. Its military is one of the strongest in Greece. Although it cannot compare with Sparta, it could contend with Athens for the second strongest. The only area in which Cornith excels is its economy, which is second to none.

Merchants from all over the world flocked to Corinth, bringing many new items and helping the economy grow in the process.

Irene voiced her thoughts, only to get a laugh from her father. There was a sense of disappointment in that laugh.

"You are indeed my daughter; your response was to be expected, but I'm still disappointed. Corinth is just as you said, but there's more. Corinth gained its strength because of its religious freedom. Our ancestors thought long and hard before making this the foundation of our power, but the times have changed."

Corinth was not built on the backs of any gods; quite the contrary. In the past, the gods were very vocal and could be seen often, but as time went on, the gods left. No one knew why the gods disappeared, but it was because of this that history only went so far back.

The gods picked their people, and they founded city-states, but none of the gods supported Corinth. This might have seemed odd, but this was what the first king wanted. Following the gods seemed smart, but only they knew how terrifying and whimsical the gods could be. The moment you worship a god, is the very moment they have control of your life.

No one wanted to be controlled, definitely not a King!

Irene did not know what to say, as she could not follow her father's trend of thought.

Not minding Irene's silence, the old man continued, "The ones who were subservient have become the masters, but we were too blind to see. The temples have infected the people within our walls with thoughts of rebellion. If we were to summon our armies to fight against the temples, how many do you think will respond?"

Surprise flickered in Irene's eyes; she suddenly understood everything. Recalling the scenes within the court, it seemed that every official believed in some god. The number of temples has grown as a result. She herself had signed off on many of those requests.

"So you are saying…"

Turning around and looking into his daughter's emerald eyes, he responded. "Yes, we need to remove the temples and those officials. I have been thinking of this since I realized it, but I do not know how to do it. The Tribunal will not allow us to destroy the temples, as that will be slapping the gods in the face. Those officials are even more difficult to remove; we do not know how much power they truly grasp. I have been an incompetent ruler and an even bigger failure as a father. I wanted to hand the throne to you without much bloodshed, but I'm not sure that I can do that now."

Irene was speechless. If her father had not said anything, she still would have been clueless. If things continue as they already were, then maybe Corinth would fall. If that were to happen, their enemies would not sit back and do nothing, especially when Corinth goes through this crisis.

Corinth did not attain its status by being peaceful alone. Rivers of blood were spilled in order to rule such a resourceful location.

Corinth was close to the Aegean Sea, the Mediterranean Sea and the Sea of Crete, gaining access to channels to trade with other powerful nations.

However, just as her father had said, no matter if they realized the issue, they couldn't do anything. Even if all of Greece fought against the Tribunal, it would be like an egg against a rock. All the Tribunal needed was a single member, and all of Greece will fall into line.

PART 2: ALMIGHTY

In an unknown location, separate from Earth and Arctara, there was a place covered in divine splendor.

Creamy white clouds roamed omnipresently through the area, with divine temples floating on top of them. A misty atmosphere clouded the unknown realm.

The faint prayers and chants could be heard within the clouds, invoking awe within the heart.

Inside one of these temples, one of the grandest, a being sat on His throne, covered in golden light, making His appearance indescribable.

No matter how powerful or how hard one tried, one wouldn't be able to peer through the gauze of the Almighty. If they did, they bore the risk of being annihilated by looking at the source of all things.

After eons, or maybe just mere seconds, the Almighty spoke to the Angel, clad in golden armor and with two pairs of pure white wings, kneeling below.

The figure looked like a noble Paladin with his lion-chested armor and long silver spear. His long, white hair spilled down with elegance. It was like how the moon reflected the light of the sun in the night, beautiful and breathtaking.

The Angel knelt at the feet of the throne of the Most High, his soul filled with piety and devotion. The honor of serving the One Above All filled him with pride.

"I have felt it, the ominous foreboding of the dark dimension. False gods have appeared in the mortal world. Their presence, while brief, could not be hidden."

The Angel's face changed slightly at his Father's words, but he could not find the words to speak. They have been fighting the dark dimension longer than he could remember, yet he has failed to see any results.

"I am appalled by this. Nothing I do seems to work. I've sealed, killed, and eradicated these false idols, and still the mortals do not hold me in their hearts. They keep causing these gods to be reborn, time and time again."

"Father, there must be something we can do. Earth will not last long if they are allowed to roam free."

The Almighty seemed to look down at the angel below, or maybe He saw everything that would be and had no need to do so.

"Micheal, my child. Whether it be Earth or that dimension, they are both my creations. The only difference is that I did not have a direct hand in the creation of the dark dimension."

A long period of silence descended, and neither of the two spoke for a while...

"I created humans in my image, but was that a gift too great? They possess a glimmer of my divinity within them, but as a result, darkness was born. Humans cannot control what they cannot see, nor can they be like us."

Micheal sighed, feeling helpless. His Father was correct. Earth was blessed with so much love and care that it cast a shadow too deep to dispel. No matter the method, the false gods would return to the dark dimension, as the mortals couldn't forget them.

God Almighty could do anything, but He couldn't defeat Himself. As long as He existed, everything else would exist. He couldn't favor one over the other; such was the love of He who sat at the beginning and the end of all things.

"However, the most concerning thing is that the Fateless One has appeared. I gave him the ability to escape our eyes, but his current actions make me wonder: Was it a mistake? Can he defeat a world that has fallen into darkness? I find this to be a disastrous task to give to one of my children, but here I sit, hoping for a miracle."

"Father, can you not restart everything and not grant humans your likeness? The dark dimension relies on the darkness of the human heart to exist."

"I cannot." Two words held heavy implications.

Micheal knew the reason but could not continue. The Dark One was weaker than God Almighty, but no mortals or idols could reach or sense His existence.

Even if He were to be erased, the Dark One would still emerge. Even if one tried, a being with the likeness of God couldn't be killed.

As long as God existed, everything existed. No one could reach His level or threaten Him. Even if they did, God would simply transcend, regaining more power.

"Fret, not my child. The Fateless One is named so, because he can perform miracles. Out of all the mortals on Earth, I choose him for a reason, but it's a pity. Becoming like us is too much for mortals. None have become beacons of light except...that is not important. Micheal, it is time for us to return. My children have fallen too far; I must put things back into the correct order."

Micheal smiled with relief. He did not mind staying between the edges of nothingness and the two universes, but it pained him to see Earth become as it was.

Without God in charge, Earth would lose its core, and darkness would descend upon it, causing problems.

Light and Dark cannot exist within the same field. This did not align with the human concept of light and darkness, where light and darkness exist within the same plane.

Light was purity and the absolute power in the universe, and darkness was the opposite.

If God were to step into Arctara, it would become like Heaven, but Earth would then become Hell. Hence, the reason they were between the two planes. However, this was contradictory as God was omnipresent, meaning He was already there. Nothing existed beyond His knowledge or His control.

God gave form to all but remained formless, like the waters that form the firmament.

God was absolutely good, but even a parent had a heavy hand at times. God was the essence of all things; hence, He was no different.

Turning around and looking into the darkness of Arctara, Micheal could feel an entity that gave him the same pressure as God staring back at him. Even he, the warrior of God, could not face that entity.

However, despite this entity's power, it never once glanced at the throne above.

No one dared to stare at God Almighty, no one!

CHAPTER 3

DIVINE FUSION

(Year 254 of the Tribunal Calendar, Month of the Virgo)

Archeus and Maria appeared in a new location with the aid of Archeus's divine power.

In front of them was a vast landmass that stretched seemingly into infinity. Tall mountains scrape the ceiling of the world, while rivers as vast as oceans divide the land.

Greenery blanketed the world, like a docile woman covering her man.

Archeus was happy with his creation. He had spent a considerable amount of time contemplating the direction of Tiamat and eventually settled on the simplest one. In a world without end, the possibilities were indeed infinite.

Tiamat was meant to be the home of the gods, but Archeus did not want it to be just that. There were many cultures on Arctara, and while not as many as on Earth, it was still a lot for all of them to coexist.

When all these cultures come together and clash, new things would emerge, changing the shape of both worlds.

Pointing a finger at the ground and lifting it up, the world trembled faintly as a temple made of jade and other mysterious metals rose from the ground.

The temple was suspended in the sky, with clouds surrounding it. It looks like an immortal palace from those cultivation novels.

Wrapping an arm around Maria's waist, Archeus flew to the temple while his thoughts blurred...

Looking at Maria from the corner of his eye, Archeus' feelings were complicated. On one hand, he wishes for her to stay with him longer because of the hole in his heart and the love she showered him with. On the other hand, he did not want her to take such a risk, but he could see her determination, and it brought him a sense of happiness.

Humans are complicated creatures. Once they get what they want, they lose interest in it or no longer want it.

Immortality...

The thing many wanted was a curse to me. My ambitions were not so great as to need them, especially the type I had.

Changing the world. Such a noble dream, but in my lifetime alone, with my power, it is more than enough to make it a reality. But eventually, even water can cut through stone.

Time would shatter the remnants of me. *Though immortal, in the far distant future, would I be the same as I am now? Will I still have these whimsical ideas and dreams? Probably not...*

This thought frightened me, so maybe that was the reason I was okay with Maria taking this risk. I didn't know...

MARIA

The closer we got to the temple, the faster my heart throbbed, and I felt a profound sense of loss.

My life has not been easy, not in the least.

In that distant land, far removed from this corner of the world, I was someone of high standing, but everything I grew to know was taken from me.

My family died, and my children and husband were burned by the flames of war. I was barely able to survive, and even then, I was branded a traitor and hunted down by my enemies.

Over the years, the hunters had shown up less and less, making it clear they were giving up, but it was painful nonetheless.

Greece was beautiful, and the people were decent... However, this was not what my heart yearned for. This was not my home.

If I had not discovered Archeus, perhaps I would have taken my life. *What reason do I have to exist? What purpose do I live for other than to meaninglessly cling to life?*

Looking at the side view of Archeus, I felt guilty and ashamed. I could sense the longing and dependency he had on me, and I had used it to my advantage.

The name 'Archeus' in my homeland meant remembrance. Through Archeus, my family lived.

I have grown to love Archeus as my own son, but the path I took to get there was disgusting.

I shook my head to get rid of the distracting thoughts. Before I knew it, we arrived before the temple doors, which swung open as if sensing our presence.

Walking inside, I was surprised to see how massive it was. From the outside, it was obvious that it was large, but I could only see its real size once we were inside.

Glancing around, I noticed Archeus cut his thumb, and a drop of golden blood emerged and floated in the air in front of me.

The blood seemed to possess incredible healing properties, as just by being in its presence, all the aches and illnesses within my body seemed to disappear.

This was not the first time I had seen this blood, yet it was a hundred times more golden and powerful than before.

Just how powerful has Archeus become? It was hard to guess.

Being able to create a world and do all kinds of feats, his power seemed to be limitless. It's a pity he claimed to be a god.

God couldn't blaspheme. There was only one being worthy of the name of God, and that was not Archeus. I was hesitant to tell him this because of his goals, but I wondered if I was wrong to stay silent?

Archeus looked at me with a worried look on his face and said, "Mother, you still have time to back out if you like. I know you want to accompany me, but this risk does not need to be taken. When I get more powerful in the future, we can try again."

Looking at the handsome man before me, I felt warmth in my heart. *Even now, my son still worries about my safety.* It seemed as if my efforts had not been in vain.

With Archeus current power, I know he was not lying. He could certainly provide me with a chance in the future, but I didn't want that.

I used him as a means to cope with the loss of my family. We both used each other, but I did not want to leave him all alone in this world.

Archeus did not belong in Arctara, he did not fit in with anyone. Even if he were to go to the land of dark warriors, he would still be excluded.

I was more of an anchor for him than he was for me. The two of us couldn't do without the other, which was why our relationship could form in such a short time.

"It is fine, I do not have much time to live anyway and I do not want to be a burden. If I survive this and can spend a little more time by your side, then it is worth it."

Archeus, you have done more for me than you can imagine, let me do something for you. We are two wounded souls that need each other to heal.

Archeus looked deeply into my eyes as if sensing something but ultimately sent the golden blood into my body.

At first I did not feel anything but as time went on, I started to feel my body's temperature rising. My blood and organs started to boil, until my flesh began to fall off my bones.

Urgh*!*

The pain was so intense that I regretted not listening to Archeus. However, I couldn't back out now, it was too late to change my mind.

My entire body felt like it was melting away, like snow under the blazing heat of the sun.

Gritting my teeth so hard they seemed like they were about to shatter, my vision darkened and my mind was on the verge of collapse.

ARCHEUS

Looking at my mother, I was shocked and terrified! *What have I done! She is all I have, what if something happens to her?!*

As I pondered about channeling my lifeforce into her body to offset the damages she was facing, a faint golden cacoon formed around her, seemingly not wanting me to do anything.

As time went on, the golden cocoon became harder and harder, looking like a golden egg with weird unknown runes on its surface.

I could vaguely hear the sound of water in the egg making me wonder if Maria was being reborn? Was her body breaking down so it can be reborn from my blood?

Wouldn't that make us biological mother and son?

After spending some time thinking, I came to the conclusion that I shouldn't worry too much. Which was difficult. I could sense the abundant life force coming from the egg, which was clear she was not in danger.

There wasn't much I could do but wait. I imagine how it would be to create a bed and take a nap... Ever since I gained my divine abilities, I could not remember the last time I closed my eyes and slept. With a body as powerful as mine and flowing with divine power, sleep was no longer necessary for me. Besides, I needed to make sure nothing would go wrong and that meant staying awake and keeping an eye on Maria.

FUSION PART 2

ARCHEUS POV

Oh? How long had I slept for? Looking outside, it is now daylight, so perhaps eight hours have elapsed, though it could be a few days since my immortal body does not need food, making it challenging to gauge the passage of time.

In the end, I gave in and created that bed. I told myself I was only going to close my eyes for a second and rest, but in no time, I fell asleep.

Scanning my surroundings, I noticed the golden egg my Mother was in was nowhere to be seen. Instead, there was a beautiful woman who looked to be in her teens floating in the air.

My efforts bore fruit, and she lived! Filled with immense relief, my heart swelled with joy; I wouldn't be alone anymore. The notion of spending an eternity with my loved ones was a prospect that anyone would cherish, let alone me.

She was absolutely gorgeous, the kind of beauty that resembled the goddesses themselves.

Since nothing seemed amiss, I left the chamber and began devising my next schemes.

My mother's transformation was too shocking to have her return to Arctara. Even with mud smeared on her face, her new appearance would be challenging to conceal.

Crista Village is a small hamlet comprising approximately 20 households and housing 50 inhabitants. Despite being established two decades after Athens, the village consisted of rudimentary structures owing to inadequate resources allocated for its development.

Farmland enveloped the village in its entirety.

In the village, the hierarchy comprises the chief, elders, guards, hunters, and general populace. The chief, aided by the elders, was responsible for formulating decisions.

With my divine power at peak capacity, few challenges were beyond me. Nevertheless, I had to discover a way to speed up the recovery of my divine power.

True Gods would be able to solve this issue by absorbing faith from their followers. Regrettably, even though I called myself a demigod, I did not possess that ability.

As Earth's literature outlined, faith consists of the redundant energy emanated by the human soul; this energy is voluntarily bestowed upon their respective deities.

Gods can harness this faith to augment their own strength. Nevertheless, should they consume the faith directed at another god, this god will become contaminated and eventually become an evil god.

In folklore, when a person dies, they linger in the mortal world for a portion of time before being summoned to the afterlife. If regrets contaminate souls, they will become ghosts and evil spirits that linger in dark places.

In theory, as the controller of the elements, I was supposed to be able to see the apparition of souls following their demise and be able to absorb these souls to increase my divine power. This was, of course, only feasible if souls genuinely exist.

The mere prospect of becoming more powerful made me think about creating a realm of souls. As a lover of fantasy worlds, the realms' appearance and regulations were things I had to think about before creating the world.

However, the most concerning thing was if I could actually absorb the essence of another being in in order to increase my own power.

MARIA

After blacking out, something transported me to an unknown place.

The location was pitch-black, suffused with intense darkness, and peppered with countless orbs of different colors in tumultuous motion.

Inexplicably, I knew what these orbs' signified; they represented the collective knowledge of every skill I had acquired throughout my lifetime.

I observed an orb that showcased images of me nursing, engaging in weaving clothing, teaching, leading, and other personal moments seen and unseen. There were things I had forgotten…

All that I was proficient at coalesced within this space.

I also understood that I must select one of the orbs to depart from this place.

Although I could not discern the rationale behind my intuition, I hesitated to select an orb, recognizing that it would affect my future.

CHAPTER 4

A GODDESS IS BORN

(Year 254 of the Tribunal Calendar, Month of the Virgo)

MARIA

"These orbs embody all the skills I have accumulated throughout my life, including but not limited to leadership, tracking, fishing, hunting, herbalism, weaving, and many others. I am uncertain which one I should select."

Drifting amidst the obscurity, I deliberated which skill to select.

Reasoning through a statistical lens, and selecting a skill that would serve me well made sense. Hunting and similar skills seemed impractical since wildlife was scarce in Greece; instead, they were mostly situated in lush mountainous areas.

After much contemplation, I decided to choose weaving. Clothing is a ubiquitous necessity regardless of location or status, with nobility being a significant market for intricately designed textiles. By replicating the attire that Archeus wore upon his arrival in this realm, I could easily gain enough money to support Archeus.

[Innate Skill Selected: Weaving.... Affinity: 7/10.... Experience: 10/10.... Alert! System issue detected... Error! Host Archeus identified... Issue remedied... Innate Skill upgraded to a Divine skill: Weaver. Scanning Host Archeus... Sub-skills manifesting... Progress: 12%, 40%, 70%, 90%, 100%. New skills created: Weave, Fate's Hand, and Temporary Spell Creation.

Divine Skill: Weaving — This ability enables the user to establish a stable channel that other entities can utilize. When honed to perfection, it grants the user the power to influence the destinies of lesser beings. However, the greater the degree of manipulation, the greater the resistance from the world.

Weave — A single-use skill that generates a magical web encompassing an area. This skill permits the user to imbue magical functions within the Weave, granting lesser beings entry to them.

Fate's Hand — Grants the user the power to modify the destiny of any entity. Nevertheless, the greater the level of modification exacted, the greater the resistance from the world.

Temporary Spell Creation — Users can fashion spells for a short duration. However, all spells produced by the user may only be temporarily stored in the Weave.

Error: Insufficient energy. Innate Divine System shutdown sequence engaged.]

The sudden appearance of the cold and indifferent voice left me bewildered and apprehensive. Without a chance to respond, I was inundated with an overwhelming amount of information that left me feeling uneasy and light-headed. Despite the sheer volume of information, I somehow managed to decipher its meaning.

The sub-skills of my divine ability, Weaving, alone made me a goddess. This was ironic since I did not want my son to pretend to be a god, but I became one.

Armed with these skills, I could help create the fantasy world that Archeus wanted.

As I opened my eyes, I discovered myself in the temple, suspended in mid-air. A sense of tranquility enveloped me, as if it were telling me I was no longer the same person.

Archeus had spoken about creating a race of Gods in the future; I supposed I was now a member of this race.

After realizing his capabilities surpassed the boundaries of humanity, Archeus decided he was a member of the God race. If he called himself a human, it would be too much. His power was too much to be labeled a human. Then again, whether it was the God race or humanity, it was just a name.

Gradually, I descended from the air and landed softly on the ground.

Although it appeared as if I descended slowly, it was just that everything around me was moving at a rapid pace, making my descent seem inconsequential.

Glancing around the surroundings, it appeared that Archeus had departed. The pitch-black skies made it challenging to discern the passage of time. Had it been a day, a month, or even a year?

"Oh my God!" I exclaimed, "My skin is so supple and stretchy. How young have I become? Am I 30 years old? 20 years old? Even younger?"

I could no longer sense the aches and stiffness in my joints. I felt I had returned to my youth.

Employing the Temporary Spell Creation, I summoned forth a Water Mirror.

From out of the ether emerged a stream of water, revealing a reflection of myself that left me speechless. It wasn't because I was unclothed, but rather because I was astonished by the stunning person staring back at me.

Now standing at 2 meters tall with the body of a goddess carved in stone and appearing just as strong. My hair was reaching below my waist and resembled the golden threads of nobles. I now met my own gaze, looking into my blue eyes, which became even more oceanic. Stunned at the sight of myself, I could only remain in awe.

I possessed a beauty that had not been seen in a millennium, a beauty that men would go to any lengths to attain. While this thought elated me, the problems that such attention could cause were not insignificant, and I would be lying if I said that didn't make me a little worried.

"I should devise a skill that enables me to create clothing," I pondered. "I cannot permit Archeus to see me in this state. After all, I am his mother."

I commenced casting the spell Cloth Creation, summoning forth fabric from the ether.

Without warning, a long, sleeveless white dress materialized before me, matching the image I had mentally crafted. Yet, I remained mindful that the dress was only temporary, existing for a mere day before it would vanish — a consequence of the Temporary Spell Creation's limited duration.

Adorned in the dress, I began to contemplate my enhanced strength. Sensing an unusual power coursing through my veins, I felt compelled to test the upper limits of my newfound strength.

"I must push my strength to its utmost limit," I pondered before crouching down and hurling myself upward with all my might. Astonishingly, I soared upwards and effortlessly grazed the ceiling, which loomed around fifty meters overhead. Such a feat clearly surpassed the boundaries of mortal capabilities.

It was no wonder Archeus decided to create a new race for them. If they still called themselves humans, even after doing this, it would be hypocritical. Although I did not feel the need to consider myself a goddess, not in the way Archeus considered himself a god, the name was adept.

As I plummeted, my mind raced with the question of how to remain afloat in the air. Suddenly, an epiphany struck me, and I cast Flight and halted my descent.

My body was suffused with a verdant glow as I hovered motionlessly in mid-air. Absent gravity, I now had the freedom to soar like a bird if I so desired.

Starry-eyed with childlike jubilation, I couldn't suppress the excited smile on my face. How many people wanted to fly in the skies but couldn't do it? Now I could easily do what they couldn't.

Eh?!

Suddenly, my head began to pulse with a searing pain, and my body became empty of power, plummeting to the ground.

BOOM!

I smacked into the ground, causing a resounding thud in the temple; however, despite the impact, I was completely devoid of pain.

It seemed that although I had become immortal and gained powers, I had not gained the vast pool of power that Archeus possessed.

CHAPTER 5

RUTHLESS

ARCHEUS

(Year 254 of the Tribunal Calendar, Month of the Libra)

One month had elapsed since Mother had melded with my blood, and still she lay dormant. Had it not been for me sensing her vitality, I would have been worried about her state of being. Nevertheless, I could sense her burgeoning might and the formidable powers she would soon command.

During that span, I constructed a temple in the Village of Cristas with the aim of acquiring faith. My objective was to determine whether the element of Yin could indeed absorb faith — an accomplishment that would elevate me to the rank of gods.

Over Element gave me command over the five elements of creation. With a series of combinations, many other elements could be born. These elements would then be separated into two: - Yin and Yang. Yin was the cold energy that existed in dark and ominous places and was represented by the moon and lunar phoenix. All females possessed Yin energy, with beautiful women possessing more of it. Yin could also include darkness.

Yang was its opposite; it embodied the light and pure energy of men, symbolized by the sun and dragons.

While these ranks were of my own making, the notion of a god possessing the ability to dominate a vast expanse of territory was not unique to my own mythological power system. Indeed, accounts in Greek and other mythologies often depict gods as imbued with such prodigious power.

Initially, the hamlets overseen by the village chief were shocked by the abrupt emergence of the temple. Despite being barred from venturing inside, the desperate plea of an intrepid trespasser proved too strong to ignore. Moved to action, I listened to his entreaty and, as a result, managed to retrieve a portion of the divine power expended in fulfilling his request.

Subsequently, as word of my exceptional abilities diffused within the villages, a group of people rose up to worship me. It wasn't long before the temple became a hub of activity, with individuals flocking to seek my counsel regarding their troubles. And while not all requests could be granted, I did manage to make my mark - healing some injuries, summoning rain, and performing other deeds befitting the ardor of my acolytes.

Through these actions, I not only strengthened my divine power but also validated the existence of faith.

Moreover, I discovered that faith was not exclusively reliant on the Yin element; indeed, it appeared that faith, a largely intangible force, could be conveyed to me from any location, even reaching Tiamat — a different dimension.

Now, I found myself ensconced within a small dimension nestled within the confines of the chapel. Being within it afforded me the luxury of observing the people and even interacting with them if I deemed it necessary.

In truth, I was keeping myself occupied with my latest project — an experiment to determine whether it was possible to bring into existence creatures from the realm of fantasy.

I realized that my blood could bestow immortality on others, as evidenced by Maria. What if I were to use the elements I control to grant someone a portion of my power?

My musings were interrupted by an unexpected visitor, a man who didn't seem older than 24 years old. He entered the chapel and prostrated before my statue. A close inspection of his form revealed a powerful physique that belied a multitude of injuries, his missing arm and the blood seeping from his various wounds being just a few of the examples.

In retrospect, my mind's eye replayed the sounds of inexplicable wails emanating from the neighborhood beyond the chapel's walls. Earlier, I thought it was a festival or some celebration, so I paid it no heed, but now that I saw this man, it seemed I was too short-sighted.

I used my divine ability over space to look at the situation, and my vision swam into clarity, granting me complete visual access to the village landscape. However, my power presented me with a grisly sight: a group of mounted men ruthlessly taking the lives of the villagers. To my horror, some of these intruders were brutally violating women right in front of their spouses before unleashing fatal violence upon them.

Even the innocent children were not spared, as they were subjected to a grotesque fate — being boiled alive and then fed to the dogs! The brutality of it all left me seething with anger. While inflicting death upon others is one thing, indulging in such heinous acts of torture is an unconscionable form of cruelty that no one deserves.

These scenes on Earth were normal, but this was not the case for this world. While I have only been in this world for a short amount of time, I could tell this was not normal. Not even the Greeks, who'd kill their slaves, would come to be this brutal.

While I continued my surveillance, my attention was snatched by the appearance of a towering figure clad in blue armor, pinpointed with a lightning bolt emblem. Concealed by his helmet, I could only discern his white hair along with an eye patch covering one eye, while the remaining eye glinted with an icily neutral expression, almost bereft of emotion.

The seated man on horseback was joined by a black-cloaked rider, who approached with haste on his own steed. The latter spoke urgently, addressing his superior, "My lord, one of our horses remains unaccounted for. Even after searching for the village, we were unable to locate it."

The one-eyed man observed his surroundings with a grim expression before fixing his gaze upon the temple, a dark and ominous gleam in his eye. "Position our men around the temple at once! We cannot allow anyone who worships false gods to escape alive!" His words were heavy with conviction, leaving no doubt about his resolute intention to eradicate anything and anyone in his path!

The cloaked man acknowledged his leader's command with a curt nod before spurring his horse towards the temple. As he rode, he let out an ear-splitting roar: "MEN! Rally to me and surround the temple! We have discovered survivors! Let no living being escape the wrath of our justice! Leave nothing alive in this den of sin and corruption!" His voice carried a tone of ruthless determination, reflecting the zero-tolerance approach of their mission.

The warriors, their blood boiling with fervor, eagerly and without hesitation, relented to their commander's command to purge the chapel of the heretics who believed in false deities.

Voices raised in an infernal chorus, they bellowed forth a deafening war cry, "KILL! KILL! KILL!" The ferocity of their intent was palpable, and the frenzy of their attack sent shivers down the spines of the defenseless "heretics."

The men, without a hint of remorse, heartlessly slaughtered any and all villagers within their immediate surroundings before making a beeline towards the temple, continuing their merciless rampage. Whether on foot or mounted on horseback, their approach was marked by the thundering of hooves and the frenzied rush of bloodlust.

I released my power, breaking its enchantment, and turned to face the man kneeling before me with an unmistakable sense of remorse. Though I had created this very temple, my actions had clearly offended some people. If there was anyone who could judge me for this, it would have to be the Tribunal.

During my research into this world, I have come across vague records about the Tribunal but did not think much of them, but it seems I was wrong to ignore them.

Faced with this situation, I knew that I had but one recourse — using my power. While I was confident that my divine abilities would allow me to easily defeat these people, the deaths of innocent villagers had left a weight of sadness on my heart. In all conscience, the least I could do was lend my aid to this man in any way that I could.

If I had just came to this world, perhaps I would not have frown if I saw this scene, but now it seems I have changed.

KAISER

A peaceful day, much like any other, passed us by as we tended to the crops and taught the children life skills. Suddenly, the sounds of hundreds of hooves thundered in our direction. The chief, ever-watchful, braced himself for a band of ruthless bandits intent on pillaging our village, but to his bewilderment, he was dealt a fatal blow as soon as the gates were breached. The sight of his crumpled form lying in two halves sent shockwaves through the panic-stricken villagers, but I knew that this was just the beginning of a brutal massacre. My thoughts raced to my wife and daughter at home, and I knew that protecting them was my top priority.

Sadly, my worst fears proved true. Even as the chief lay dying, hordes of mounted men began to pour in, unleashing a bloodthirsty killing spree that showed neither mercy nor discrimination.

Absolutely anyone who came in their path was met with gruesome violence, no matter how defenseless or innocent they might have been.

Devastation and horror gripped me as I finally reached the biggest hut in the village — the one I shared with my family. The sight that greeted me was nothing short of a nightmare. My precious wife, the love of my life, was being brutally assaulted by these unhinged men. Worse still, my innocent daughter was being forced to witness this unspeakable act of violence. I could see from the multiple bruises and traumatic signs on my daughter's body that they had already committed unspeakable atrocities before I arrived. It was like my entire world had shattered and crashed down around me.

My mind went numb with rage and disbelief at the heinous scene unfolding before me. My precious daughter was barely 9 years old, still so innocent and pure, and yet these savages had forced her to bear witness to their despicable acts. What manner of beasts could even contemplate such atrocities? I wondered in anguish. Even the vilest demons of ancient lore had some sense of boundaries and limits, but these men appeared to possess none.

Overcome with immense fury and unable to bear the sight before me any longer, I drew my sword and charged at the two men assaulting my family. With every fiber of my being, I pushed myself to the absolute limit, driven by a blinding rage that threatened to consume me. In a blur of steel and bloodshed, I struck down those inhuman monsters, ensuring that they could never hurt my family, or anyone else's, ever again.

In the intense frenzy of battle, I sustained a grievous wound that would haunt me for the rest of my days. One of my hands was completely severed from my body, leaving me writhing in agony that seemed almost unbearable. With every passing moment, the searing pain seemed to grow more intense, like a thousand needles piercing through my flesh. Despite the torrents of anguish that threatened to consume me, I knew that my family needed me now more than ever. Settling into a grim determination, I tried my best to rise up once more and face the horrors that were laying ahead.

Torn between shame and rage, a cold fury overtook me as I gazed upon my family's violated bodies. In an act of desperate defiance, I began to disrobe my wife and daughter, gently removing their ravaged garments before carefully dressing them in the clothes of the two men whose lives I had just brought to an end. Though their garments smelled of sweat and blood, I knew that this was the only way to preserve what little dignity they had left. As I tenderly wrapped them in their new clothing, I promised myself that I would do everything to keep them safe and avenge the atrocities that had been committed against them.

As I stumbled through the rubble and carnage that was once my home, a terrible realization dawned on me: these attackers had not simply stumbled upon our village by accident. Their grim determination and ruthless efficiency spoke of meticulous planning and preparation, suggesting that they had gathered intimate knowledge about our community and its people. The sickening thought that these assailants had kept an accurate count of our village's inhabitants filled me with a sense of dread and foreboding. It was then that I knew that this was not some random act of violence but rather a calculated and deliberate assault aimed at destroying every last vestige of what we held dear.

Picking my wife and daughter up, I put them on the back of the horse and let them leave the village.

As my family rode away from the safety of the village, disguised as members of the invading army, I couldn't help but feel a flicker of relief, knowing that they had a chance at escaping the horrors that awaited them. Though my heart ached as I watched them grow smaller and smaller in the distance, I knew that their safety was the only thing that mattered at that moment.

Finally, with a sense of purpose and determination, I descended upon the temple - the last bastion of hope for our people. Braving the dangers that lay ahead, I prayed that I could somehow turn the tides in our favor and honor the sacrifices of those who had already perished.

In my heart, I held a steadfast conviction that a divine presence was watching over the humble temple that had become our refuge. With every passing day, my faith grew stronger as I witnessed the small but miraculous blessings that the deity had bestowed upon us — from life-saving rains to miraculous recoveries from sickness. Every time I raised my voice in prayer, I felt that the benevolent god was listening to my pleas and answering them. Believing in the unwavering power of his divine grace, I knew that we could still emerge victorious, even in the face of the most formidable challenges.

As I crept through the village, my heart shattered at the sight of my dearest friends falling one by one. Despite the agony of helplessness and the urge to intervene, I knew that every move I made posed a significant threat to my own survival. With a heavy heart, I had to acquiesce to the limitations of my power and instead find solace in my unwavering trust in the divine providence of God, Kris. In the face of unimaginable peril, I summoned every ounce of my courage and strength to keep moving forward towards the temple.

The excruciating pain that wracked my body paled in comparison to the ache in my heart as I staggered forward. Once I reached the sanctuary, I dropped to my knees in desperation and prayed with all my might, my voice trembling.

"God of Wishes, Kris, I humbly implore you to save our village from the horrors that have befallen us. I am willing to offer everything, even my own life, for the sake of our people. Please hear my plea and grace us with your divine intervention!"

With tears streaming down my face, I could only hope that my fervent prayers would reach the ears of the benevolent deity and move him to act in our favor. Amidst utter despair, I clung to the unwavering faith that God Kris would respond in ways beyond my wildest expectations.

In a voice resonant with power and divinity, the deity spoke, promising me deliverance from the nightmare that had engulfed the village.

"I shall bestow upon you a power that no mortal has ever wielded. And in return, I ask only one thing: that you defend your people and rid your land of the evil invaders who seek to conquer and destroy. Your righteous fury shall be the instrument of their defeat, and your enduring faith shall preserve the souls of your fellow villagers."

ARCHEUS

The epithet given to me by the villagers resonates strongly in my heart; they call me the God of Wishes, Kris. Though this name was not of my own choosing, it had become a source of joy and pride for me, a reflection of my deep affinity for the people of this village.

Using my real name from Earth would have been imprudent, as it did not conform to the sensibilities of this world. The name Archeus could not have come at a better timing.

The timing couldn't have been better. This individual has arrived to provide me with the raw materials I need to create a new race. I had been contemplating this for a while, but I was still struggling to gather the necessary resources. Now, the possibilities were endless. Given the current predicament, the creation of a new race, one that offers a formidable defense against our enemies, was imperative. The logical conclusion that I have reached is that the Vampires or the Werewolves would have been the ideal candidates for this endeavor.

The backstory of these creatures was often shrouded in darkness, but what could be more foreboding than having one's entire home razed to the ground? Their formidable capabilities, including accelerated healing, enhanced strength, and other extraordinary powers, have instilled a deep sense of fear and trembling in the hearts of other creatures. This provided me with an excellent opportunity to augment my divine power by presenting myself as the God of Fear, a manifestation of the terror that these creatures provoke.

Emotion is a potent source of energy, just as faith provides a wealth of energy to gods. If an individual were able to assimilate the fear and other intense emotions of the masses, they would be capable of harnessing an extraordinary degree of power, perhaps even ascending to godhood. Each intense emotion they would absorb would contribute to their ascent into divine status.

Through intense concentration and a singular focus on the Yin element, I channeled my power toward the man.

The cost of this transfer was substantial; a significant percentage of my divine power dissipated, flowing directly into the recipient's body.

I was surprisingly shocked to notice that the loss of divine power I lost was permanently gone. Maybe because I was giving this man a part of my divine ability instead of blood like Maria. There was still so much I did not know about myself or my power.

CHAPTER 6

CHANGES

(Year 254 of the Tribunal Calendar, Month of the Libra)

MARIA

After just a few days, I had already mastered many of the powers bestowed upon me, though my control was still not perfect.

Through the use of Temporary Spell Creation, I could now produce an impressive variety of spells that allowed me to create almost any effect I desired. That being said, I had to admit that there were still limitations to my newfound abilities. Despite my rapid progress, during my experimentation with Temporary Spell Creation, I also uncovered a few weaknesses, aside from the spells' inherent time limitations.

Temporary Spell Creation had certain limitations when it came to producing exceptionally powerful spells, as anything beyond a certain limit would fail to condense in spell form. I had once attempted to create a Casualty Spell, but Temporary Spell Creation did not even react.

Even though I was supposed to be the controller of Fate, I could not use Temporary Spell Creation to create Fate-related spells.

The Weave, after being released, spread across Tiamat, and I thought it would be contained, but my fears did not come true. The Weave broke through Tiamat and entered Arctara.

Through the Weave, I could perceive an invisible energy that began to emanate, slowly spreading across Tiamat, encompassing Athens and its surrounding regions.

I was able to use the energy as if it were a part of my body.

Within the Weave was a mysterious, twelve-layered pyramid that appeared barren of any physical matter. Each of these layers could be accessed from any location throughout Tiamat and Athens. The power to connect with the Weave was dependent upon one's mental fortitude; the more potent the mind, the greater the capability to gain entry.

Opening my hand, I looked at a crystal tower rotating with mysterious energy. The tower was divided into twelve layers, each as vast as a world. This tower was the physical manifestation of the Weave. Once a spell was integrated inside, it would be archived inside the crystal tower.

I was not the only one who could put spells inside the Weave. If someone created and put a spell into the Weave, the Weave would place it on a layer and reward the individual with a significant infusion of the mysterious energy. As the possessor of the Weave, I would also be provided with a portion of this energy, which would improve my divine power.

For someone who possessed such a small pool of divine power, this was tailor-made for me.

Eh?!

Using the Weave as my eyes, my focus descended on Arctara, looking at the temple inside Crista. Unlike my normal eyes, I could see anything I wanted within the field of the Weave. My senses could feel everything; it was like I was there in person.

Gazing intently upon the scene in Crista, I got to witness Archeus creating another world that was different from Tiamat. It was dark and ominous, but since the Weave had not spread to it, I was not able to see inside. However, it was only a matter of time before it did.

Apart from the new world, I was more curious about a humanoid figure. What attracted me was the similarity between Archeus and the figure. Unlike Archeus, who, in my perception, was filled with power, the figure seemed to possess only a faint trace of it.

After some time, I decided to retract my gaze and begin ruminating on my next course of action. It dawned on me that I had attained power that many would long for, and yet, beyond being in Archeus' company, I lacked any discernible purpose for it.

It became increasingly evident to me that Archeus was serious about his plans. He has talked about making the world more interesting and bringing purpose to the majority of Arctara. What I did not understand, however, wasn't creating more creatures with his power making the world more chaotic?

I introspectively pondered whether Archeus' objectives had undergone a change or if this creation served some obscure purpose within his grander scheme, which eluded me.

One thing was certain: maybe Archeus did not realize it, but he had changed. Was his power what changed him, or maybe he was always like this? If it's the power that caused those changes, will I change as well? I had numerous questions but lacked answers for any of them.

PART 2: QUESTIONS AND UNDERWORLD

ARCHEUS

When I transferred my divine power into the man's body, a noticeable transformation occurred. Although his height remained the same, other alterations took place — his regenerative capabilities kicked in, allowing his missing hand to regrow. Furthermore, his physique naturally rearranged itself into an optimal form, facilitating a more agile and nimble build.

The transformation of the man continued to take shape as his formerly blonde hair grew lighter, eventually settling on a shade of pure white. His eyes underwent a similar shift, now a deep, striking black, and his once-rounded ears became pointed. The finished result saw him appear as an otherworldly prince of the night, exuding a type of charm that few mortals could hope to rival.

A cursory glance at him was all that was required to match his features with those of a common fantasy race, the Dark Elves!

As my Yin element began to flow through the Dark Elf, it acted as a channel, gradually instilling within him the very essence of this race.

The enormity of what I had achieved left me stunned. Instead of shaping the specific creatures I had sought, I unintentionally birthed an entirely different, rare entity — a Dark Elf. Known for their cunning ways and often regarded as malicious, I couldn't shake the sense of surprise that washed over me.

While it was uncertain if this Dark Elf aligned with the popular portrayal often found in fiction, a sense of anticipation inside my body continued to grow. From the shadows and in absolute silence, I would observe their every move, attuning myself to their strengths and weaknesses as they navigated this world of ours.

The emergence of this Dark Elf had significant implications. Not only did it require me to further solidify my status as a deity among men, but I would also need to oversee the careful creation of more of his kind. It was vital that he engage in mating with humans, allowing for the continued evolution and propagation of the Dark Elves.

The creation of another Dark Elf seemed highly impossible, considering the current one was a mere byproduct of an unintentional mistake on my part.

As the Dark Elf had originally arrived to safeguard his wife and daughter, I felt a sense of responsibility to see his quest through to its conclusion. Despite them leaving the village earlier, I could utilize my abilities to track them down, giving him the chance to reunite with his loved ones. Given my contribution to the events that had led to his present circumstances, it seemed only appropriate to offer a helping hand.

"Mortal, I have bestowed upon you the power to fulfill your deepest desires, and in doing so, you shall transcend your former human self, henceforth existing as the first Dark Elf in this world." Yet, as the notion of godhood crossed my mind, I wondered if there might be a more suitable path forward. Rather than assuming the mantle of a new deity myself, why not grant that title to the Dark Elf, allowing him to assume the mantle of God of the Dark Elves? After all, he had become the very embodiment of this unique and rare race.

My own experimentation had left me with no doubt about the existence of faith and its ability to augment one's divine power. In the case of the Dark Elf, not only did he already possess a portion of my Yin element, but he also possessed the potential to father more of his kind, who could then worship him as a deity. The combination of these factors made it entirely feasible for the Dark Elf to ascend to godhood.

After careful assessment, I've determined that the Dark Elf's current strength falls slightly below that of an Ancient, yet noticeably surpasses that of most individuals possessing the Gift. To accurately classify his level of aptitude, it would be appropriate to refer to it as "Half a Step Ancient."

Despite my beliefs, it remained unclear whether the acquisition of the Gift would indeed bestow upon one a range of mystical abilities. At this point, my conclusions remained purely speculative.

Given the limited extent of my divine power, estimating the number of individuals who may have acquired mystical powers proved to be a challenge. The outcome was difficult to predict with certainty.

The notion of attaining deity status lies beyond my comprehension. Based on my understanding, achieving this elevated rank would have necessitated amassing a vast number of devoted followers. However, the initial requirement was to attain the top-tier status of a demigod.

This possibility hinged on the assumption that his potential matched that of mythical elves. Without confirmation of this notion, it seemed conceivable that he might never surpass the level of Ancient in his lifetime.

Although this sequence of events might have appeared time-consuming, it occurred within a matter of seconds in the real world.

"Mortal, I recognize that I have caused you considerable pain and suffering, and I wish to make amends. As the God of Wishes, known to you mortals as Kris, I possess the ability to grant wishes and am therefore both a god and a demon. Through my actions, I have inadvertently brought forth a new being in the form of yourself, and with further mortal interaction, it is conceivable that a new race could arise. In recompense, I offer you a portion of my godhood, specifically dominion over darkness. With diligence, you could ascend to the position of a god, with subordinate deities under your control. Enough discussion; do you accept my proposal?"

Observing the stunned expression of the Dark Elf before me, I couldn't help but smile within the alternate realm. In truth, I anticipated his agreement — after all, who could refuse the prospect of becoming a god, even with potential obstacles and entanglements along the way? A moment of pain for an eternity of blissful existence is a trade that even the most foolish would embrace without hesitation.

As I spoke, I was surprised to find that I had unconsciously figured out a way to become a Primordial God, even though the level of gods still eluded me.

By bestowing a portion of your power upon another being, any subsequent increase in the amount of faith that they absorb would in turn augment your own power. Through this process, you would experience continual enhancement over time. The strength of your subordinate gods had no bearing on this progression; in actuality, the more powerful they'd become, the greater your own potential for growth would be.

Pursuing this train of thoughts, when I granted Maria my blood, it stands to reason that the same principle should have applied. By imparting my blood within her, she could have grown increasingly powerful with each new individual that would choose to worship her. In turn, this would result in a corresponding increase in my own power.

However, that was just a theory. There was a clear difference between Maria and the Dark Elf. One was created through my blood, and the other through my divine power. Creating others with my blood had an advantage, while using divine power was a much weaker method. It even caused the divine power that I used to be permanently gone, without the possibility of recovering it.

In many ways, Maria was distinct from the Dark Elf. For one, she possessed immortality, an essential quality to assume the mantle of a goddess. Additionally, she wielded considerable physical strength beyond that of humans. Considering that my blood coursed through her veins, I wouldn't have been surprised if Maria had even acquired some of my own powers.

Godhead refers to a unique authority or power possessed by a deity, such as the power to create fire or manipulate time. In various mythologies, gods were depicted as rulers over specific laws or domains in the world, an ability that was beyond the reach of mortals.

As such, godhead was a relatively weaker concept, as it did not possess the same magnitude of power as ruling over a law or aspect of the universe. It could be viewed as a more accessible power, one that was easier to acquire or understand.

Only Primordial Gods could use aspects of the universe on their own. Even though they had 'god' in their name, it could also be assumed they were on another level altogether. They didn't have any of the limitations the gods had.

The Dark Elf responded without hesitation, displaying a hint of slyness in his words. "Oh, mighty God of Wishes, Kris, I would be honored to become a god. However, I presume there are additional motives for you wanting me to become a god. After all, it seems unlikely that mere guilt would prompt a deity to bestow godly status upon someone."

A flicker of surprise lit up my eyes, but the feeling of happiness soon followed. Life would be boring if I had complete control over everything. It was the variables that brought excitement and made things interesting. Perhaps these variables could have even given rise to my polar opposite, indirectly shaping the meaning of my existence.

"There is a specific reason I have chosen to elevate you to the status of a god. The world is heading towards greater chaos, and none of the deities can freely descend from Tiamat due to the world's restrictions. I intend to cultivate a god in this world to exert some influence. It is a mutually beneficial scenario for both of us. With your ascension, more people will become aware of the God of Wishes, while you will obtain divine status, resulting in a win-win situation."

These statements were all lies, of course. In reality, there were no other gods in this world aside from myself and Maria. Ascension was a make-believe concept that held no weight since no gods existed. Nevertheless, as power became increasingly concentrated in the hands of individuals, it was likely that the world would be unable to withstand such forces. To prepare for this eventuality, I have fabricated the notion of ascension from the start. By convincing this Dark Elf that becoming a god is a real possibility, I could guide future generations of potential gods to believe this falsehood and perpetuate the myth.

"What are the possible consequences? Is there indeed a world that exists beyond our own?"

I found it difficult to respond to his questions. For one, I would have had to confess that the transformations we perceived were of my own doing; as creator of the Dark Elf, I also hoped to bring vampires, werewolves, and — perhaps even — magic into reality. In effect, this world would have gradually shifted towards the manifestation of my ideal fantasy-driven environment. Secondly, being a modern individual, I was aware of many worlds within the universe of Earth, so the answer would have been yes. I had no doubt that the Dark Elf was inquiring whether or not Tiamat was a reality.

"As time passes, a substantial number of people will grow substantially more powerful, and the journey towards godhood will be open to many. Moreover, not only does Tiamat exist, but the Underworld does too, and there are scores of other enigmatic secrets lying hidden. However, it is critical to note that without achieving godhood, attaining this knowledge could ultimately be your downfall."

The Dark Elf took a moment to think about it before answering, "I undertake to popularize your name, and I give you my word that the Dark Elves shall flourish as a result. You can trust that I, Kaiser, the future God of the Dark Elves, will deliver on this vow."

"Very well, I shall await you in Tiamat. Take caution, however, as the temple is currently encircled. Regrettably, I can no longer exert my influence on this world, so I bid you farewell — at least for now." I ceased speaking and quickly employed my divine abilities to turn invisible, leveraging the Yang element to bend light around to mask my presence, springing unobserved above the nearby village.

Observing the situation first-hand was very different from using Time and Space Control to observe the scene. The sight before me was truly grim; countless women and children were being mercilessly killed by their captors, while even the men were suffering a horrific fate, succumbing to mutilation by horses.

While this was occurring, a portion of the mounted men suddenly charged towards the temple, their eyes now a deep blood-red hue. They resembled a pack of ravenous wolves that had just caught whiffs of the most delectable prey in the world.

The rage that I had been suppressing grew even further, and I had to take a deep breath and count to ten in order to get it under control. My existence couldn't be known right now. Even though my actions have undoubtedly caught some attention from the Tribunal.

"With Kaiser attended to, my next task is to assist those who have perished." Impressively, my divine power reserves have expanded twofold since my last endeavor, granting me the energy reserves of a true god.

Regrettably, the one thing I still lacked in my pursuit of godhood was godhead.

Initially, it was perplexing as to why I had not attained godhood, despite possessing an ample reserve of divine power. The answer, however, was rather straightforward: I had yet to impart to myself the necessary godhead. Not only that, I was not a real god but someone who possessed great power.

The qualities of faith and godhead were pivotal to attaining godhood. Although I might not have been pursuing divinity in the traditional sense, I still needed my own unique brand of godhead that specifically pointed to me as a deity.

The concept was akin to when I assumed the guise of the God of Wishes; I was able to successfully receive veneration from followers, both owing to the absence of other deities of similar monikers and due to the power of Faith driving their devotion towards me.

To elaborate, even if I were to pretend to be Zeus, I would be incapable of attaining his followers' faith since I was not truly Zeus.

What this meant was that I must simply bestow myself with a godhead with border coverage, and in doing so, garner a large pool I could absorb faith from.

I had an idea for my godhead, but I was hesitant to solidify it because once I accepted the godhead, it would have been hard to change. Even then, if the followers were not aware of this change and still worshiped me as a different god, I could be contaminated and become an evil god.

Shaking my head, I opened my palm and used Time and Space Control to create a realm with the Yin element being the primary element.

Creating a realm was quite easy, far easier than one would think. Honestly, as long as I had a thought and if it was feasible, my divine abilities would make it happen. It was truly user friendly.

Inside the palm of my hand, an infinitely vast void manifested, absorbing the divine power feeding it.

A parcel of land materialized, progressively expanding in size. A deluge spouted from beneath the soil, causing massive flooding around the world. Mountains emerged and ascended towards the highest altitude of the realm, eventually culminating at its very summit.

A rift in the fabric of reality manifested at the apex of the mountain and began to whirl without hesitation.

A ghastly veil of darkness enshrouded the entire realm, rendering it ominous and foreboding. Volcanoes erupted that spewed cold energy instead of fire and lava. A huge moon sat firmly in the sky.

I grinned as I gazed at the Archeron, the underworld of my fantasy world. A fantasy world that does not have an underworld cannot be considered a fantasy world.

I gazed down at the Village of Cristas with emotions flickering through my eyes. This place might have been recognized for all the lives that were lost, yet several significant events have originated from here. Perhaps, in the future, this would become a hallowed site.

It was a pity that these people died, but my actions have undoubtedly fueled this.

Just like Tiamat, the Archeron expanded in tandem with my divine power. Therefore, any individuals who perished in the vicinity of Athens would have their souls sucked into Archeron.

Despite the fact that I couldn't see faith, I could vaguely sense its existence, and my growing divine power was proof of it. With the Yin element, seeing souls and ghosts was not impossible. However, with Archeron being made primarily of Yin, did it have the ability to absorb souls? Or did *I* need to absorb the souls actively?

Releasing the world within my palm, it rushed behind layers and layers of space and began to expand rapidly, reaching the same size as Tiamat.

As the creator of both realms, I could sense their location without issue, but that might not have been the case for others.

Within the confines of the Archeron, located on top of a mountain, a rift in reality began to spin, giving rise to an unseen and inconspicuous suction that rapidly spread in all directions.

As the suction continued to grow, individuals located in the region of Athens sensed an icy chill coursing through their bodies, as though something was attempting to suck them in. As swiftly as the sensation arose, it dissipated into nothingness, just as the suction began to shrink and gradually assimilate the souls of the deceased.

The souls appeared astonished, glancing around with a palpable degree of confusion. Some of these souls had been lingering around for numerous years after failing to arrive in the Underworld. They bore witness to the fate that befell souls who lost their will to continue, fading away into nothingness.

Realizing there was no world beyond death, numerous souls lost their faith in the gods, and with it, their hold on righteousness. They transformed into malevolent spirits, with a few of them possessing sufficient strength to temporarily influence Arctara.

Yielding to the beckoning of death, these souls relinquished any resistance and manifested atop a mountain, at which point the surrounding darkness granted them physical forms.

These souls were taken aback; the world enveloping them was a far cry from the depictions of the afterlife in the myths. They were bereft of the boatman and the Tartarus they had heard of in tales, instead sandwiched between a world of tranquility and a silence that was nearly overpowering.

It appeared as if this world had either just been born or abandoned. The souls realize that they might be on the outskirts of this new world.

Gazing upon the scene transpiring within the Archeron, a wave of relief washed over me.

With the Archeron now operational, I could find solace in the possibility of a potential revival, even in the event of my downfall.

After pondering for a brief moment, I resolved to infuse Archeron with a sense of novelty and purpose. If Archeron remained nothing but a holding chamber for the deceased, bereft of notable beings, it would slip into the background, powerless, before the fickle machinations of the gods in the times to come.

Suppose Archeron boasted its own military unit; in that case, it would furnish a potent counterforce capable of challenging the gods, possibly dissuading them from taking the underworld lightly.

The competition served as a catalyst for growth, as it motivated individuals to strive for betterment.

Having decided to initiate communication with the souls, I had to adopt an identity in preparation. Although this would only be a one-time introduction, I had to make it impactful. Hades was not an option, as it could lead to complications down the line in case other gods were privy to this. Hence, opting for originality was the ideal course of action.

Through the utilization of my complete control over Archeron, I succeeded in projecting my voice across Archeron, reaching every new soul.

"Listen, dear souls. I am Adis, the Lord of Death, and I have utilized the very last iota of my divine power to manifest a new realm specifically to safeguard your souls. As the world metamorphoses, the number of souls inhabiting it is predicted to multiply exponentially. Thus, this is my final gift to this world. Farewell." I declared, flinging a pitch-black rock skyward, eventually landing atop the mountain's summit.

At the resounding echo of my commanding voice, the disoriented souls whirled around in disbelief before falling prostrate to the abyssal ground. My identity left them awestruck, rendering them trembling on their knees.

The souls were flabbergasted beyond words, knowing they had been transported to a realm of death and were in the presence of the divine. To them, anyone who could create a new world must be a god; thus, they dared not show any disrespect, acknowledging their subservience.

The black rock was the corporeal manifestation of Yin itself, and if somehow obliterated, the power it would unleash could equal that of a demigod's full strength.

Craved on the rock was some information and an ability that could help promote the growth of Archeron.

Although my intrigue weighed heavily upon the Kaiser versus Holy Warriors confrontation, I was impelled to make haste toward Maria's whereabouts. It had been a full month since I last surveyed her situation, curious as to whether she had finally regained consciousness or perhaps offered other developments. Nonetheless, I urgently needed to visit and examine the situation firsthand.

PART 3: LIGHT VS DARKNESS

KAISER

As I knelt, I implored the divine being to safeguard the few villagers remaining. My confusion deepened as I failed to understand why these assailants had descended upon us. This world was a desolate and pitiless place for the ordinary and destitute populace, with the gods ignoring our mere existence.

Tears streamed down my face as I bellowed out in the direction of the only deity I knew: "Mighty God of Wishes, Kris, I plead unto thee, rescue our imperiled village. I would forfeit everything, including my life, in the pursuit of this salvation."

Despite my screams, I harbored no expectations of a divine response. The prospect of my own mortality was of little concern to me, for I had already reconciled with how vain the gods were.

Perhaps it was the overwhelming sense of fear and disorientation that compelled me to hear a voice that appeared to emanate from all directions, yet nowhere in particular.

"I will rescue you and offer you unmatched power. In addition, I will safeguard the souls of your fellow villagers. All you need to do is eliminate the invaders."

I was certain I had not misheard. The voice was undoubtedly present! But were the gods genuinely here, or was this an impersonator looking to test my devotion before eliminating me? I've heard similar tales often in the past.

As in Greece, Rome was believed to have multiple deities, and yet, a faction of priests started preaching about the existence of one supreme being, causing outrage among the populace who have lived with a myriad of gods for centuries.

Aware that they couldn't afford to infuriate the people beyond a certain point, the priests intermingled with the common folk but gradually met their demise as they stood by while helplessly watching their sacred items get desecrated.

Could it be that these warriors were employing a similar strategy? No, that didn't appear likely, given their determination to eliminate everyone in their way. Hence, the only reasonable explanation would have been that the voice actually belonged to a true god — the mighty deity of wishes, Kris!

As I knelt down, a rush of energy surged through my body, instilling within me an immense sense of power. It was an inexplicable sensation, as though I could single-handedly uphold the weight of the heavens. Even though I knew it was impossible, I could feel my physical being grow increasingly powerful.

Before my astonished eyes, the missing arm regenerated, and my vision began to heal and improve, along with my old wounds. My hair turned pure white, and my skin slowly darkened, leaving me in awe of the profound transformation taking place.

As I surveyed the surroundings, I could feel the darkness enveloping me, almost inviting me to embrace it. Conversely, gazing at the light outside the temple, I was overcome with a sense of loathing.

I couldn't resist smiling despite all of the pain. I was aware that even though I gained incredible power, I had also surrendered much. Although I could no longer walk under the sunlight like I had until now, I knew the sacrifice was worth it. Giving up the sunlight for such immense strength was a no-brainer.

As I basked in the admiration of my newfound power, a chilly, almost detached voice resounded in my mind, bringing forth a sense of calm and urging me to understand my newfound gifts.

[Non-human entity detected... Dark Elf identified... Presence of the Divinity of Yin discerned... Generating racial skills... Acquisition of Night Vision and Extended Life confirmed... Initial attempt at Bow Mastery unsuccessful... Error detected... Solution found... Processing Divinity of Yin... Acquisition of Shadow Walker and Dagger Mastery confirmed to compensate for weaknesses... Identification of racial vulnerability to Sunlight, Low Fertility, and Low Physical Body... Initial remedy unsuccessful... Solution found... Immediate Physical Body acquired.

Racial Skills:

- Night Vision: Enables the user to see with clarity in darkness, irrespective of any obstructions.

- Extended Life: Allows the user to live three times as long as a human being.

- Shadow Walker: Grants the ability to teleport through shadows in complete silence, making the user's movements undetectable by normal means.

- Dagger Mastery: Enables seamless wielding of a dagger, where the user adopts the dagger as their own entity.

- Racial Weaknesses:

Include a susceptibility to Sunlight, reducing the user's abilities by half when in its presence, Low Fertility, lowering the chance of offspring by threefold, and Immediate Physical Body, though remedied by immediate acquisition of enhanced strength, twice that of an average human.]

I was easily able to understand what the voice was saying as the voice spoke in a manner that I could understand. The voice explained the extent of my newfound power and the abilities that accompanied it.

While among humans, I possessed indomitable power, in the eyes of the gods and other higher beings, my strength might have as well been the same as a human.

It's quite a realization that I am now classified as a Dark Elf, no longer burdened by my mere humanity. Although, I couldn't claim to sense any substantial difference except for the notable surge in power.

"Mortal, I recognize that I have caused you considerable pain and suffering, and I wish to make amends. As the God of Wishes, known to you mortals as Kris, I possess the ability to grant wishes and am therefore both a god and a demon. Through my actions, I have inadvertently brought forth a new being in the form of yourself, and with further mortal interaction, it is conceivable that a new race could arise. In recompense, I offer you a portion of my godhood, specifically dominion over darkness. With diligence, you could ascend to the position of a god, with subordinate deities under your control. Do you accept my proposal?"

The words spoken by the God of Wishes left me bewildered. *Could it be that achieving godhood was truly that effortless?* In Greece, the number of individuals who were believed to have accomplished this feat is less than ten, and even then, their ascension was shrouded in mystery.

Nevertheless, at this moment, an authentic god has offered to bestow divinity upon me; it's no wonder that I am astounded.

As I regained my composure, I realized something peculiar. No matter how many mortals perished, even if it was at the hands of the gods themselves, no one would raise their voice in protest, myself included. Well, not explicitly. If their lives meant so little to the deities, why extend this gift of godhood? Was this transcendence not as desirable as we mortals perceive it to be? Or did it come at a cost, some form of constraint or affliction?

The reasoning of the God of Wishes eluded my comprehension, but that was expected, for he was a deity. If it were possible for a mortal to decipher his rationale, then the essence of godhood would lose its significance.

After substantial reflection, I concluded that accepting the offer was the right thing to do. At this point, I had no reason to turn it down. Even if it turned out that it was a curse, it wasn't too late to break free from it by ending my existence. "Oh, Great God of Wishes, undoubtedly, it would be a privilege to become a god, but I am certain that you have other motives beyond guilt, for nobody would believe that a god would give away godhood solely out of remorse."

Things didn't seem to add up, which implied that there must have been an alternate reason for the God of Wishes to make me this offer. I was confident that my life wasn't in any danger, and even if it were, battling a deity was an insurmountable task. After all, a deity was deemed a god because it transcended mortal abilities.

A hint of appreciation could be sensed from the god's voice: "I have a motive behind bestowing upon you godhood. The coming times are fraught with chaos, and none of the gods can descend from Tiamat because our powers are too overwhelming for this world. I intend to cultivate a deity in this realm to exert some influence before you ascend. In this manner, we both stand to benefit. A greater number of individuals will become aware of the God of Wishes, while you will ascend as a god — a mutually beneficial arrangement."

While spreading the name of Kris was not a terrible proposition, I couldn't help but feel that there must be more to it than that. Despite my desire to believe otherwise, the pieces don't fit together all too well. Spreading a name could be done by anyone; it didn't require becoming a deity to do it.

Before committing to godhood, I had to determine what Kris truly wanted and assess the potential risks. As I was reflecting on Kris's words, it appeared that there could have been other worlds beyond our own, but was such a notion even feasible? As far as I was aware, according to history and the lore that I have learned about, this world was the only reality. Even fabled realms like Mount Olympus and the Underworld were believed to be situated within our world.

"What would be the consequences of ascending to godhood, and is there indeed another realm beyond our own?"

"As time passes, a greater number of individuals will amass significant power. The path to godhood will become accessible, and countless people will attempt to achieve it. Moreover, Tiamat isn't the only realm in existence. The Archeron, the underworld, is a tangible place where the souls of the dead dwell. Other secrets abound, but without ascending to godhood, possessing such knowledge can prove hazardous to you."

Was this world more complex than it appeared on the surface? The appearance of a deity surely confirmed that something peculiar was transpiring. What could have caused the world to be this way, and why is it undergoing these changes now of all times? Could there have been someone surreptitiously manipulating events behind the scenes, and if so, what would have been their motives?

"I accept the responsibility of spreading your name and vow to ensure the prosperity of the Dark Elves in the time to come. As the future deity of the Dark Elves, I, Kaiser, pledge to devote myself to this cause."

"Understood. I'll await your arrival in Tiamat. The temple is under siege, and my influence over this world wanes. Farewell, for the time being."

With the weight of Kris's aura lifted, I stood up and brushed the dust from my clothes before making my way outside the temple.

At the temple's perimeter, my gaze fell upon the foe that threatened the Dark Elves' future — a radiant, glowing ball of fire looming ominously above.

Utilizing my racial skill, Shadow Walker, I vanished and materialized within a nearby shadow. Once there, I scanned the troops encircling the area.

Every warrior wore a cloak concealing their armor, although an occasional gust of wind would rustle their garment and reveal the immaculate white armor underneath, gleaming brilliantly in the sunlight.

Several warriors remained mounted on their horses, while others dismounted and stood ready on the ground, brandishing their weapons.

Their eyes shone with a manic fervor, brimming with both madness and exhilaration as they trained their gaze upon me.

Beyond the ranks of warriors, a massive figure on his horse caught my attention. Though he stared my way with a cold detachment, there was something undeniably menacing about his eyes that sent a shiver down my spine.

Thankfully, the man's attention departed from me, directing his gaze skyward with a look of bewilderment.

As I gazed upon the warriors, I detected a palpable aura of malevolence, rife with thoughts of destruction and murder. Had I not maintained a firm grip on my psyche, my consciousness could have been overpowered by an animalistic, primal urge to escape.

Huff!

I took a deep breath, exhaling slowly to help myself focus. My attention turned towards the warriors, and as I counted their numbers, I noticed there were now around 70 soldiers remaining — fewer than the hundred I'd seen at the start.

Does that mean the others are currently slaughtering the village? The thought churned within me, stoking a fiery anger in my heart.

With the aid of Shadow Walker, I materialized beside an unprepared warrior and deftly twisted his neck, rendering him lifeless. I promptly liberated his sword from its sheath, readying myself for the next confrontation.

The moment the blade landed in my hand, foreign memories flooded my consciousness, granting me knowledge of not just swordsmanship but also the intricacies of wielding the slender weapon as a dagger.

Easily weaving between the shadows, I materialized behind and in front of the warriors with deadly intent, dispatching them with little resistance.

The warriors' shouts and frantic weapon swings proved futile against my relentless attack. Even when they loosed volleys of arrows in my direction, I'd materialize amidst the archers themselves, swiftly eliminating them.

As I fought with unmatched strength and dexterity, a troubling thought crept into my consciousness. If my current prowess - only twice that of a human - was already considered a weakness, what then must a fully empowered elf be capable of? Or could there be some hidden aspect to this division of strength I have yet to uncover?

I was lost in thought when I saw the large man shouting and rushing in my direction on his horse.

Throughout the battle, I had fixed my gaze on the imposing figure of this man, whose very presence seemed to exude an overwhelming pressure upon me. The sensation mirrored my interactions with Kris, a powerful pressure enveloping me.

The gravity of the situation was not lost on me, for the man's power was nigh comparable to that of Kris, a god. It stood to reason that this man had to be a demigod, as that was the limit of strength the world could endure.

The realization that I might have to face off against a demigod sent a wave of apprehension coursing through me. I knew that my current levels of strength and training left me ill-equipped for such a showdown. My newly acquired abilities were undoubtedly powerful, but mastering them would take time and discipline, luxuries I might not have been afforded given my current situation.

Contemplating my limited options, my mind turned to the possibility of an escape. Given my weakened state, possessing barely a third of my previous energy, my best chance was to utilize the trusty Shadow Walker to slip away. However, this maneuver was not without risk, for if it were to fail, I would be stranded without any other means of escape.

With Dagger Mastery on my side, I was assured of my safety in most close combat scenarios, and this understanding lent me some measure of reassurance. However, relying solely on one skill to escape was risky business, and the thought of potential failure weighed heavily on my mind.

Another factor that I had to consider was the time of day. While it's currently daytime, my powers would be greatly diminished in the absence of Shadow Walker, effectively halving my strength. This meant my chances of escaping with minimal damage would be further reduced without the aid of this crucial skill.

Questions began to race through my mind at breakneck speed. *What kind of powers did a demigod possess? Were they powerful enough to nullify my skills or, worse, dispatch me with a mere thought?* The more possibilities that I considered, the more apparent it became that I was dealing with an entity far beyond my current comprehension. Though vengeance burned within me, I knew that recklessness would only lead to disaster. Before I could make a move, I needed a better understanding of his capabilities.

The man calmly approached on his horse, locking eyes with me.

Twenty meters felt uncomfortably close. Without hesitation, I triggered Shadow Walker, disappearing into my shadow and leaving the man behind without a trace.

What Kaiser did not realize was that, the moment he left, the area he was standing on was now completely obliterated, the ground beneath having been effortlessly sliced away with a single sword slash.

PART 4: HOLY WARRIOR BORAK

BORAK (LEADER OF HOLY WARRIORS)

Perched atop my horse, I surveyed the advancing ranks of Holy Warriors with a pensive expression. My mind was consumed with the latest orders issued by the Three Stars of the Tribunal, and I found myself lost in thought even as my troops marched steadily onward.

As a proud member of the Tribunal, I held myself to the highest standards of loyalty and integrity. Though some of the tasks I have undertaken on their behalf have been less than savory, I have remained steadfast in my devotion to their cause. The Tribunal's actions, no matter how harsh or unforgiving they may seem from the outside, were always carried out with the loftiest of intentions: to nurture and safeguard our world.

I needed to remain level-headed and objective at all times, regardless of how I felt. To let emotions rule me would have been tantamount to abject failure in upholding my duties and could even lead to incalculable harm for those I strived to protect.

The sheer number of souls that have met their end at my hands easily dwarfed even the most violent chapters of Greece's storied history. Given that I had existed in this world for well over a thousand years, it stood to reason that I was privy to ancient knowledge and esoteric secrets that few others even knew of, let alone comprehended.

Under its veneer of simplicity and apparent mundanity, this world was a place of unfathomable danger, where even the mightiest of gods could be killed at any moment. The fact that it appeared so ordinary and unremarkable was a testament to the current dearth of divine activity, with only a small handful of deities remaining actively engaged in the affairs of mortals.

Bound by a solemn oath not to interfere with mortal existence, the gods themselves had no place in worldly affairs. Any deity who should be so rash as to break this sacred vow faced not only severe retribution but even the possibility of their own downfall. As such, the Tribunal existed to act as the gods' conduit to the world, enacting their will and carrying out their divine mandate.

The Tribunal served as the mortal realm's foremost mouthpiece for the pantheon, possessing both peerless strength and a fearsome array of divine weapons to carry out their commands. As the vanguard of the gods' will on Arctara, no obstacle — be it mortal or godly — can truly hope to withstand their might.

In a world where the divine weapons of the Tribunal hold sway, few factions dared to invite their wrath by opposing them. Even those who harbored ill will for the Tribunal could do little more than sit idly by and seethe, for to actively attempt their removal or destruction would be to risk awakening the ire of the gods themselves. Simply put, the Tribunal's supreme power was enforced by the sheer magnitude of their divine might and the fear that came with it.

As per my mandate, there is presently an evil deity lurking in these lands, seeking to supplant the worship of the native gods with blasphemous, foreign pantheons. This presented an existential threat to the very fabric of our beliefs, for should our gods be forsaken and forgotten, the repercussions would ripple far beyond the here and now. In this case, the cost of inaction far outweighed the potential consequences of intervention; we had to act swiftly and decisively to protect our faith and avert calamity.

It was an immutable fact that the gods formed the bedrock upon which our world was founded. Whether they are benevolent or malevolent in nature, the power and influence they wield can't be denied. The passing of any deity was a grievous blow to the delicate balance of the world, for each one represents an irreplaceable piece of the divine puzzle that sustained our existence. To lose even one is to invite danger and uncertainty into our midst — a truly perilous state of affairs.

Long ago, the untimely demise of Poseidon, God of the Sea, had cataclysmic consequences for our world. In the aftermath of his passing, a great flood swept across the land, reshaping the landscape and claiming countless lives. The impact of his absence was felt not just by the survivors of the flood but by all the inhabitants of the world. With one less deity to preside over its natural elements, the delicate balance of nature was thrown into disarray, leading to further chaos and upheaval. Ultimately, the loss of Poseidon had a profound and lasting impact on the world and its people, leaving them forever altered in its wake.

Many of the city-states that once adorned this world were washed away, never to be seen again.

While Evil Gods may share certain qualities or abilities with the gods, it would be fallacious to conflate the two as interchangeable entities. Evil Gods do not share the same benevolent nature or adherence to morality as their counterparts and often seek to sow discord or destruction wherever they go. Though their powers may appear similar on the surface, their motivations and priorities are vastly different. It's crucial to differentiate between the two to avoid being misled by superficial similarities.

Although mortals possess a certain degree of power, it is challenging to kill a god, as the gods possess abilities and strengths that exceed mortal comprehension. Even if a god is seemingly defeated, an Evil God can regenerate with the power of faith. However, gods are not impervious and can be vulnerable during periods of weakness, such as when they first ascend or when the faith of their believers wanes. In such instances, it may be possible to strike a fatal blow. It is essential to recognize these nuances and act accordingly when dealing with gods, for failure to do so can result in dire consequences.

Another method to bring a god down is to eliminate all of their believers and erase their memory from the world. By doing so, the god would lose the foundation of their power — faith — and fall into a state of powerlessness. This method, though extreme, is a surefire way of bringing down even the most powerful of gods.

With my sword in hand, I peered towards the heavens. A curious sensation rippled through the air, as though some unseen force had disturbed it. Though I scanned the area intently, I detected no immediate signs of danger.

Shifting my gaze away from the heavens, I directed my attention towards the nearby temple. As I watched, an unfamiliar figure emerged from the entrance and began to make their way towards me. The identity of the man remained a mystery to me, and I braced myself for whatever might come next.

The architecture of this building bore a striking resemblance to those found in barbarian lands, a place I had visited on prior occasions. Its unique design elements were distinct from anything that would typically be found in this part of the world.

In contrast to the many gods worshiped in other lands, the inhabitants of barbarian land exalted a single deity that rivaled even the might of Zeus. My mind wandered, and I couldn't help but ponder the possibility that the faithful in this area may have been influenced by the teachings of Roman priests who fled their homeland to propagate the belief in the one true god.

The deity worshiped by the barbarians has long had its sights set on Greece and the surrounding areas. Its followers - sent in the form of messengers and priests - have attempted to convert the populace to their beliefs but have met resistance at nearly every turn. Despite this, evidence suggests that some have indeed succumbed to their efforts, creating a growing problem that is difficult to reign in or even detect.

Should this temple indeed be of barbarian origin, it would seem that their god was now poised to claim the worshippers of the Greek pantheon as their own. The presence of this temple on Greek soil signaled a significant shift in the religious landscape, and it remained to be seen how this would impact the people of this region.

As I watched the figure emerge from the chapel, I found myself growing increasingly perplexed. The being in question did not resemble either a barbarian or a human and appeared to hail from an entirely different realm altogether.

Barbarians shared a human-like appearance, possessing a humanoid physical form. Their skins were both durable and taut, typically displaying a deep, durable brown shade. However, what set them apart from humans was their animalistic strength and demeanor. Their most distinctive attribute was their ability to wield Beast Magic, which tapped into the power of their animal companions to unleash a formidable source of energy.

To mortals, the man before me might have appeared as nothing more than a mere human being, their vision limited by the constraints of the mundane world. Yet to me, his otherworldly constitution was immediately apparent. His body was so much more than that of a mere human — it had been transformed and altered beyond the natural realm. The sheer intensity of his life force blazed bright, like that of a scorching sun. Despite my own stature as an almost immortal being, I couldn't hide my surprise.

Given the vibrant strength of his life force, one could easily assume that he would live for centuries without interruption, were it not for the capricious nature of fate. Looking at his life force, I could see he had not trained, meaning his lifespan could increase further. *This is truly fascinating!*

The implications were clear; there was no denying that he was a humanoid creature, belonging to a race that possessed striking human-like features yet was demonstrably distinct from humanity in every other way.

In this world, a vast array of sentient beings exist, some possessing intelligence beyond that of humankind itself. Nevertheless, the vast majority of these creatures have either been captured and subjected to research or sealed away due to their overwhelming power.

My eyes widened in horror as I watched the man nimbly leap from one shadow to the next, his movements almost too quick to discern. With cold efficiency, he cut through my knights as though they were no more than vegetables on a chopping board.

My amazement knew no bounds! It was clear that the creature before me was not a demigod, yet how could he manipulate the laws of nature with such ease? For someone to do so, it required not only prodigious intelligence but also the necessary life stage, a feat I myself had been unable to achieve yet.

Without possessing both the required intelligence and the necessary life stage, one could never hope to ascend to the demigod realm. It was precisely for this reason that so few had managed to achieve such a feat over the ages, their numbers few and far between.

Within this world, the path to strength was divided into six stages. Beginning with Mortal, one could progress through Transcendent and Legend before reaching the elusive realm of Mythical. Above that lay the domain of the demigods, and those who truly succeeded in their journey of strength could attain the ultimate pinnacle: the realm of the gods.

Gradually, my brow furrowed in consternation as I watched the number of warriors dwindle down. While I had little regard for the majority of my warriors, I knew I could not allow my Vice Captain to fall at the hands of our adversary.

The Vice Captain was among the select few within his generation to possess the potential to become a demigod. To lose such an individual in this battle would be nothing short of a devastating loss.

Even within the esteemed Tribunal, there existed a mere five demigods, which included the Three Stars. This number was far lower than what we had in the Age of Gods.

Demigods reigned supreme as the second most powerful beings in the world, positioned a mere step away from the domain of the gods. Yet, despite their lofty status, the journey from demigod to god was an insurmountable one, only achievable by the most exceptional of individuals.

Becoming a god required not only the comprehension of a law but the presence of devoted followers as well. However, with the gods already using all mortals as their own pawns, it was impossible to ascend to godhood without first gathering one's own following.

In the event that a new god were to ascend, the consequent weakening of many other gods would also pose a threat - there existed a genuine risk of a god falling from grace. Mortals, after all, could only produce pure faith for a single deity, and attempts to spread their devotion amongst several gods would only lead to fragmented and less potent faith.

Usually, there would be festivals on a set day of the week or month because the faith of mortals is not infinite. It needs time to recover.

As I observed the number of men dwindling further, I spurred my horse into action. Failure to take action while the warriors of the gods fell in battle would not only lead to my own downfall but also incur the wrath of the gods themselves.

The longer one treaded upon this path, one would become more acutely aware of the true terror that gods instill.

"RETREAT, MEN!" Bellowing, brandishing my sword, its demonic luster gleaming in the light, an eerie reflection of the countless lives it had taken.

Still riding my horse, I initiated a heartfelt prayer: "Patron Gods of War, Athena, and Ares, lend me thy divine grace and bestow upon us the War Grace we need!" In an instant, a mystical power surged forth and enveloped the remaining warriors, doubling their strength and speed.

The warriors, feeling the increase in their power, did not choose to fight but instead fled the scene. Despite their sharpened strength and augmented speed, deep down they knew that in the face of absolute strength, they would still be defeated.

They did not understand the power of their enemy and could not anticipate when they would be the next to fall. They clearly had more experience and strength, but they could not use it effectively.

As the Vice Captain made his speedy escape, I was admittedly relieved, yet my disappointment at his inability to vanquish such an evidently weak opponent lingered still.

Even after having reached the Legend stage, his complete inability to put up a fight was a clear indication of his inadequate training thus far. It appeared that I would need to intensify his regimen even further.

Looking down at the enemy, a sudden shock reverberated through my being. Though the distance had obscured my perception before, it was now undeniable: this creature possessed a trace of divinity. *I pondered, how was this possible? Divinity was supposed to be exclusive to the offspring of gods, the demigods.*

Divine force was the fundamental tool utilized by the gods themselves to traverse the world when they wanted to mingle with mortals.

Given the limitations imposed by their immense power on mortal bodies, the gods often opted for incarnation by possessing human vessels. However, to protect themselves in the mortal world, wherein the physical limits of human forms left them vulnerable, divine force was developed.

As a demigod, I existed in a state of being intermediate between the divine force and law energy. Only when the entirety of my energy has been fully transmuted into that of law energy would I qualify to transcend into godhood. And yet, this transcendence required faith to be achieved.

Remarkably, this implied that the man in question skipped many stages and only needed time to reach or even surpass my level. Just eat and sleep to become a god. If anyone heard this, everyone would laugh in sadness and envy!

Yet the mystery lingered: which god had sired a child into the mortal world? It seemed unlikely that the God of the Barbarians was behind this, leaving the question unanswered.

It was unlikely that the God of the Barbarians was responsible for siring a child into the mortal realm, as such an act would result in an overwhelming loss of divine energy. No god possessing ambition would be foolish enough to leave themselves vulnerable in such a state of weakness.

As a solitary god, the God of Barbarians would hardly make such a novice mistake. If the news that he had sired a child were to spread, many other gods would doubtlessly seize the opportunity to claim his godhead and absorb his divinity, leaving him vulnerable and weakened.

No matter how much I was yearning to uncover what transpired, my mission remained simple: to eliminate the threat, not to gather intelligence.

"Although your origins pique my curiosity, your fate remains unchanged," I muttered nonchalantly as I gripped my sword tightly with one hand before the 'man' that stood in front of me.

It had been eons since I had last engaged in combat, for few could endure the sheer power of the Borak, the God of Oblivion — not even a demigod could.

Different from the prayer to the gods, once the sword was unsheathed, a blood bond materialized, imbuing it with the capacity to channel both divine force and law energy.

As the sword swung towards the 'man', everything vanished into nothingness. Before the sword's edge, hope, space, and time itself ceased to exist!

Such was the ferocity of this assault that even a deity would incur severe injury if they were not prepared.

A smile crept up my face as my intuition signaled that the 'man' had evaded my strike.

Not bad.

Although I was intrigued by the 'man' and had no intention of slaying him, if he lacked the ability to handle even the most basic of strikes, he had no reason to live.

"Fascinating," Despite the strike being simple, that designation applied solely to entities of tremendous power. Any opponent lacking in might would find my maneuvers, whether involving Oblivion or not, insurmountable.

The Path of Oblivion coursed through each of my attacks, infusing them with its very essence, erasing all existence swept up in their wake.

One would scarcely recover from such a wound, for it would gradually devour every essence of their being until nothing remained.

While it was a pity I had chosen this path, I could not change it. If others had the chance to become a god, I would not be included in that list. The path of Oblivion required everything to be destroyed; there was no way the gods would ignore this.

While I was gazing upon the sword's incision, a figure caught my eye. I glanced to my side to see the return of the Vice Captain.

"My Lord, have you slain that man? He was a dreadful sight. How can one possess such strength yet exhibit such clumsy movements?" Inquired the Vice Captain.

My Vice Captain was right, and I knew it. The man was undeniably skilled, but his clumsiness had gone unnoticed in the heat of the moment. How careless of me!

However...

Staring coldly at the Vice Captain, I spoke authoritatively, "He is no more, for no entity can withstand my assault imbued with the very Law of Oblivion. Elias, however, I must express my disappointment. You have trained beside me for 50 years, and yet you couldn't best a mere novice? Your training will become harsher from here on."

Elias's face was drained of color. "My Lord, you misunderstand. I believe I could engage him one-on-one in combat, but that strange power of his is hard to counter. If he chooses to flee, I can scarcely touch even the hem of his garment."

"I will hear no excuses. Instruct our men to gather all valuables and set the village ablaze, endeavoring to present it as an assault from bandits. Dispose of the fallen warriors' remains by burning them."

Vice Captain Elias sighed loudly as he proceeded to carry out his orders.

Dismounting from my horse, I entered the temple, astounded by its modest proportions. It consisted of a single room containing a one-meter-tall bronze statue of a deity, the god's outstretched hands inviting all in a welcoming embrace.

One of the statue's hands clutched a lustrous apple, while the other grasped a withered and decayed fruit.

Inscribed upon the statue's base were the etched words, "Kris, God of Wishes."

"The God of Wishes?" I murmured aloud. "Then it was not the God of Barbarians. Nevertheless, an unknown deity poses an even greater threat."

At the very least, the tactics and behaviors of the God of Barbarians could be understood. For this god, everything would be start from scratch.

Looking at the statue and balling my right hand into a fist, I shattered it.

Leaving the statue might cause unseen problems if someone happens to start worshiping it. The reason for coming here was to remove this tumor. The slaughter of the villagers was just a part of it.

With no purpose left to linger in the area, it was time to depart.

I made sure to survey the inferno that was devouring the village before turning away and riding off into the fading rays of the evening sun.

As I set out, I could feel a pair of eyes that looked at me with anger and deep hatred. I could reach out and kill him, but I felt it would be interesting to see how his character would develop.

Should this man harness his hate to ascend to greater levels of strength, then it would justify his continued existence.

CHAPTER 7

GODHEAD

(Year 254 of the Tribunal Calendar, Month of the Libra)

Upon returning to Tiamat, Archeus looks for Maria, curious about her current condition. Had she acquired some of his powers and become immortal like him? Regardless, he felt elated at the prospect of seeing her again.

Inside Tiamat, Maria found a room to claim as her own.

As she settled at her desk, Maria detected Archeus's presence, though she remained uncharacteristically muted. Uncertainty gripped her, unsure if Archeus had realized the corruption wrought by his power or if he remained unaware of its impact. The state of her son evoked memories of a dictum she had learned early in life: 'Absolute power corrupts, absolutely.'

Even if someone is unaware at the moment, upon reflection, they will realize they have become corrupted.

Archues was surprised to not see Maria at the location he left her, but it did not take long for him to figure out where she was. He appears before her, studying her intently.

Her golden hair flowed like golden solar flares, radiant, while her deep blue eyes, similar to the ocean, shone with wisdom and purity. Maria's skin was white and free of any blemishes. She was simply gorgeous.

Maria has truly become a beauty that could be considered unparalleled throughout history.

Archeus could sense a slight power waffling off her body. Though it was not as intense as expected, he could feel it.

Maria reciprocated his gaze, sensing a newfound weight emanating from Archeus's body. The air hummed with an aura of godhead, the likes of which only the most powerful figures possessed. Even while maintaining stillness, Archeus commanded a gravitas beyond expectation. *How had he achieved this transformation in such a short time?* She wondered in dismay.

She also thought he always had this power, but she simply could not sense it. Although she was not actively using the Weave, her senses have changed.

"Mother, how do you feel?" Archeus asked as he sensed a shift in Maria's demeanor, making him wonder if something was bothering her.

"I feel strong and invigorated, unlike before," Maria replied, a spark lighting up her eyes as she spoke. "It's as if an endless reservoir of vitality flows through me. Maybe only time will tell, but I think I might possess immortality."

A smile of relief formed across Archeus's face. Maria had not only attained immortality but had also grown in strength, a promising sign. The next question on Archeus's mind was if she had gained any divine abilities.

Without being asked, Maria offered a thorough explanation of her newfound abilities. "I now possess the power to shape the flow of fate, along with some supplementary skills."

Archeus quietly listened to her, surprised by all the information she was disclosing.

As Maria spoke of her powers, Archeus' mind began to connect the dots. He came to the realization that he might have been summoned to this world by the so-called 'Innate Divine System', which enabled him to create creatures like Kaiser and divinities like Maria. The system had empowered him and allowed him to grant portions of his abilities, allowing him to assist characters he encountered.

Archeus found himself growing increasingly bewildered. *What was the purpose of the Innate Divine System? And why had it not provided me with any missions?* Maria's words had confirmed his suspicions that the system was incomplete, leaving him with a new series of unanswered questions. *What can I do to complete the system?*

Forcing his mind to stop generating an infinite thread of new questions, Archeus directed his gaze to Maria. He couldn't hide his happiness. Through creating the Weave, she had established a crucial element in any fantasy world — the possibility of actual magic. It was no longer just an elusive concept, but a genuine reality to be explored.

However, he was once again confused. *The Weave is something that is seen in Dungeons & Dragons, but why did Maria gain it? Where does the Innate Divine System gain its power from?* There seemed to be a layer of mist covering everything.

Things might not have been as simple as they seem.

"Thank you for sharing this with me. Now I know what my path forward should be," Archeus expressed with gratitude. As the possessor of the Innate Divine System, he held the power to create fantasy creatures and divinities. Yet, it occurred to him that since there is an Innate Divine System, there must also exist an equivalent danger in Arctara.

Archeus recognized a theory he had encountered through virtual reality: the more powerful a system, the more dangerous the world.

Although Earth was ruined, there were still many remnants left over. Virtual reality was one of them; although it was not something many people sought, Archeus was not one of them.

That was why, even though the term 'System' came up, he understood it without issue.

As he reflected on his past actions, Archeus couldn't help but feel a chill run down his spine and a slight sense of fear. With the existence of Holy Warriors in the Village of Crista, there is a high possibility the gods were real.

What if a real god had attacked him? Would his immortality save him? The unknown was frightening, and the gods were unknown.

Was it confidence the reason he overlooked the Holy Warriors, or was it arrogance in believing no one could reach his level? Archeus was not sure why his behavior had slightly changed. He has always been a cautious and calculating person, but with these powers, his mind seemed to have changed.

On Earth, if he lowered his guard even slightly, he ran the risk of dying. But here with Maria, his guard has lowered.

However, it was clear that he was exposed to the gods. He did not have the element of surprise. They probably knew him better than he knew himself. After all, he did not hide his power because he believed the gods to be figments of people's imaginations.

Sighing, Archeus found himself with a long to-do list, locating the Holy Warriors at the top of his list. Their ability to uncover his whereabouts, despite his efforts to cover his tracks, indicated that there existed a powerful force capable of tracking him down. He couldn't help but speculate that the gods themselves might have aided the Holy Warriors.

Secondly, Archeus planned to establish a way for people to become Mages now that Maria created the Weave. He already had an idea, but it is rough and needs to be perfected over time.

Finally, the last one was to locate the gods themselves.

Archeus yearned to acquire the knowledge that only they could offer, considering that they had been in existence for ages and their wealth of experience was invaluable.

There were many things he could not understand, such as why he was brought to this world. Archeus was not stupid enough to believe that the system just brought him here with no purpose. The ability to create fantasy creatures was awesome, but for what purpose did that serve the system? Also, it did not seem that the system was the one who gave him his powers.

If you were to think about it, he had three powerful abilities that could make him a god to mortals, but those did not compare to the Weave. The Weave's potential was very high. As long as the Weave continued to exist, Maria could easily reach the level of true god or even above that.

Many things were going through Archeus' mind. If the system could grant such power to Maria, why was it still inactivated? Plus, it was clear the system had no effect on Archeus, meaning it was not behind his current power. Which meant something or someone had to be responsible for it, but why? That was the concerning part.

Her voice was filled with confusion when Maria spoke, "Archeus, I've been thinking a lot lately. After obtaining the Weave, I've been closely monitoring you, and I've noticed a change in you. Are the words you spoke to me mere lies? Why did you give that person your power? Can't you see that it will only bring chaos? Doesn't that go against everything you've been striving for?"

He didn't sense Maria spying at all. Was this a feature of the Weave? If it were someone else, they might have been concerned, but not him. He did not have anything to hide from her. Otherwise, he would not have given her the opportunity to be by his side.

Archeus could sense that Maria was beginning to doubt him, and understandably so. He couldn't deny that he had indeed changed and possessed enormous power.

The fact that he had managed to restrain himself from causing chaos was remarkable.

He knew he would change but was sad it was so soon. The change was so subtle that, without reflecting and examining himself, it would have been hard to notice.

Maria could notice this change, mainly because she has been close to him for the last three years.

He couldn't deny what Maria had just said. He created a Dark Elf, which would indeed turn this world into chaos. He knew that very well, but he still did it. And if he had created a Vampire or Werewolf like he wanted, the danger would have only been greater.

But, despite everything, he did not regret his decision. This change was needed to propel this world to one that would be able to survive longer than Earth. If the price he had to pay in order to do this was his sanity, then so be it. At the very least, this world would be one Maria could live in; that was enough.

"The reason I wanted the common folks to change their destinies was you, Maria. You possess a heart of gold and always lend a helping hand to those in need. But that's just not me. I have never been selfless, and it was impossible to be so in the world I came from. Everyone had to fight for themselves, and relying on others meant putting your fate in their hands." While he did not want to ruin the image she had of him, Archeus was not stupid enough to pretend for eternity to be something he was not.

He was from an eat-or-be-eaten world. If he were a goody-toe shoe, he would have died. The number of people he has killed to survive was enough to scare her. It was already a miracle to come out of that without becoming completely ruthless. To pretend that he was good on top of that was hypercritical.

Maria was at a loss for words. She understood what Archeus had said all too well. It was a universal truth that living solely for oneself was already challenging enough, let alone for others. Sacrificing oneself for another seemed far beyond what she was capable of, and she pondered whether she would ever be able to do so.

"I apologize, Archeus. You are not from this world, so you bear no obligation to assist it. Your creation of the Underworld is already a significant contribution, yet here I am, being critical of you without doing anything myself." Why should Archeus sacrifice himself for people who never fully accepted him in the first place? It would be a senseless act. After all, everyone had their own degree of selfishness, and no one was perfect, even when helping others. It was a self-centered act, as it was driven by the notion that someone needed help.

Maria couldn't help but feel that even when she had rescued Archeus, it was out of her own need for companionship. She had helped him, but it was also a way for her to alleviate her loneliness.

"Chaos is not my goal; it is a byproduct of the process. The reason why the world is in such disarray lies with those in positions of power. The rulers dictate what the world should look like, and it is the same everywhere. The strong enforce their will on the weak. What I'm suggesting is: Why not become one of them and exercise your own will? You want everyone to be content, and this can only be achieved by possessing strength." What Archeus didn't mention was that granting people freedom was actually detrimental to the human race. What would be considered freedom? Allowing everyone to have unrestricted control over their lives? But wouldn't that put others in danger, thereby taking away their freedom? Governments limit freedom because, without it, the world would descend into anarchy. Humans are sinful creatures, and once the barriers that they have been hiding behind are removed, they'd become beasts that would do anything to satisfy their desires.

When Archeus suggested that Maria impose her will, she was caught off guard. It wasn't what she had in mind, but to achieve her goal, it seemed like the only solution. However, she wasn't naive. Maria knew that if she imposed her will, it wouldn't solve the problem; it would simply replace the leadership while leaving the underlying issue intact.

Perhaps if Maria approached the situation from a different perspective, it could yield fruitful results. As a goddess with dominion over fate, she was no longer a mere mortal.

With a gradual and cautious approach, Maria believed that she could ultimately achieve her goal of creating a world of authentic freedom.

Upon seeing the realization settle on Maria's countenance, Archeus knew he had accomplished his objective. He was certain that this discussion would have transpired sooner or later, regardless of whether he had desired it or not.

Bestowed with immense power, Maria was bound to entertain certain thoughts that could potentially lead her astray. Although these musings weren't inherently malicious, they posed a risk.

Archeus realized that if Maria coerced him into behaving as per her desires, he would cease to be his genuine self, which was counterproductive. He hoped for an authentic relationship, with both parties reciprocating and supporting each other.

In addition, he was aware that his mother held a traditional view that deemed females inferior to males. Despite his efforts to convince her otherwise, this belief remained entrenched. However, by declaring her a goddess, Maria transcended this limitation and broke free from these limiting conventions, thereby becoming more formidable.

Materializing in his room, Archeus reclined in a meditative posture. Although this technique differed from the practices depicted in cultivation novels, it served the same purpose of promoting mental clarity and fostering visualization skills.

With the existence of the gods in this realm a possibility, he realized the pressing need to enhance his capabilities and ascend to the level of a true god at the earliest opportunity.

He had already devised a plan regarding his godhead. If he was at all correct, once his godhead was acknowledged, anyone worshiping his divine name or his godhead would serve as fuel for augmenting his divine power. His declaration as the 'God of Wishes' was a testament to this fact, as faith poured in from all corners, propelling his divine power.

Upon ascending to the rank of true god, he would acquire yet another layer of immortality, augmenting his existing level of immortality by a trifold.

He had been blessed with Eternal Vigor, granting him the benefit of enduring true immortality. Archeron had granted him protection against death, as long as his soul remained intact. Additionally, his godhead bestowed immortality upon him, which would exist as long as mortals worshiped him.

His lack of vulnerability was not questionable, as he could only be vanquished if his existence was destroyed three times, repeatedly. But since he was not sure about Eternal Vigor, it was possible even the gods couldn't breach this level of immortality.

When he first questioned the level of Eternal Vigor, he got a vague feeling that he was beyond death. Even death couldn't claim him.

However, since his method of gaining divinity was not orthodox, he was still feeble in the presence of true gods.

According to what he knew about true gods, they exhibited an unparalleled mastery over rules and laws, to the extent that their power was virtually unfathomable. The notion of a true god possessing the ability to obliterate an entire continent single-handedly ought to be unsurprising. However, the most glaring weakness concerning gods of faith was their reliance on mortals.

The moment you'd kill the followers of a god, that is the moment they'd fall. No matter how powerful they'd be, they'd be unable to escape this fate.

So while he was still weaker than them, it was not hard to see which one was better. At the very least, he had freedom. Whether he had followers or not, he couldn't be affected.

After careful and thorough introspection, Archeus opted for the godhead of omnipotence, the one he believed was best suited for him. He refused to limit his boundless potential, as his power held limitless possibilities. With such vast capabilities at his disposal, there were hardly any feats he could not accomplish. Additionally, selecting a more restrictive godhead would mean he would have to cope with impending limitations, which he was intent on avoiding at all costs.

As he was contemplating, he once again realized that his godhead paled in comparison to the power the gods wielded. They both had godheads, but the difference between those born as gods and those who acquire godhood was very glaring.

If his creativity was good enough, he could bridge this gap and stand on equal footing with the gods.

Archeus closed his eyes, allowing the divine power within him to condense as he visualized the image of his godhead. As he concentrated, a vivid image of his godhead began to materialize within his mind, revealing itself to him with an almost blinding radiance.

Inside his mind, a brilliant glow of light spread far and wide before contacting and turning into a purple sapling.

On the sapling, a small fruit with mysterious runes could be seen.

The sapling began to absorb the divine power inside Archeus's body, growing taller to the naked eye. The sapling became a towering tree whose height couldn't be examined. The fruit was golden and pulsing like a heart.

Archeus' body, which was empty of divine power, began to recover as the fruit spewed out divine power, which was ten times more pure and even stronger than it was before.

While power surged through his body, the tree sat firmly in his mind, absorbing divine power and spewing out purer and stronger power for Archeus' use.

The surprising thing for him was that the new divine power was easier to control than he expected. Not only that, he could use all his divine abilities without any difficulty. While he could do this before, it was not to this degree.

With his current strength, Archeus imagined he could destroy at most half of a continent. He was technically a true god, but he was not a genuine god. A true god, a real one, could destroy a continent with ease, but he could only destroy half of that with all his strength. The difference in strength was obvious.

He was surprised at how easy it was for him to ascend and become a true god. If this were those cultivation novels, he would have faced tribulation and spent months in seclusion, but in reality, not even a few hours had passed.

With the power surging through him, Archeus didn't feel as hopeless as he had before. While there was still a distance from the gods in his mind, the number of things he could do only increased.

At the very least, he was no longer just a demigod.

Because of him, Taimat had obtained its first true god. Maria was still a demigod. Even if she did not decide on her godhead, when the Weave reached its absolute limit, she would not stop at a mere true god; she would only aim higher.

With his growth in divine power, Tiamat and Archeron underwent a massive expansion, gradually spreading until they enveloped more than half of the Northern Highlands. Consequently, he found himself imbued with the vast powers of omniscience and omnipresence, enabling him to survey and govern over vast swathes of territory and many of its cities under the coverage of Tiamat and Archeron.

As they expanded, the boundaries of Archeron brushed against an unknown area isolated in layers of space, making Archeus ponder about examining it. However, since there was a more pressing issue, he made a mental note so he wouldn't forget about it and descended to Arctara.

CHAPTER 8

WAY OF MAGIC

(Year 257 of the Tribunal Calendar, Month of the Taurus)

ARCHEUS

Since my ascension three years ago, several significant events have occurred. Above all, the difference in our values and aspirations had strained my relationship with Maria; she had grown more aloof and wholly committed to the study of Fate, leaving little room for our prior closeness.

It turned out that women were very complicated, even as goddesses.

Secondly, Maria's creation of the Weave led me to add numerous spells to it, which had taken more than two years to create over thousands. The spells I created were quite diverse, ranging from minor spells, like Fireball, to forbidden ones, like Heaven's Fall.

Although this entire process was boring, it was helpful for exploring the limits and understanding my divine abilities more clearly.

Thirdly, when confronted with a daunting task, I've learned that it's best to seek help. Despite my considerable power, what I could achieve still had limits. Although my godhead would suggest otherwise, the fact remained that I couldn't do everything alone, and beyond Maria, there was no one else to turn to.

This, in turn, made me eager to create more gods. Well, this was not because I did not have anyone to help me, but because of my concern about the gods of Arctara. With just Maria and me, standing firmly would have been a difficult task to achieve. Even if I didn't want it to happen, if the gods turned out to be my enemies, I would be defenseless before a large group of beings with power surpassed me.

From where I was standing, it looked like the gods were more of an enemy than friends, if the Holy Warriors could be interpreted as the mouthpiece of the gods.

Once magic is widespread, it will herald the beginning of numerous possibilities, and my interference will gradually become less necessary. The only people I needed to be concerned about were the gods, but I didn't think the gods would disagree or be mad because of the changes I planned to bring.

After all, in a fantasy setting, that is when the gods were truly powerful. If mortals kept advancing as they were, eventually they would stop believing in the gods, and the gods would eventually fall.

In the past three years, I discovered Eternal Vigor had a hidden function: body modification! As long as I had an idea of what I wanted to be, whether it be a woman or a man, I could use my divine power and Eternal Vigor to make it happen. However, my taste was not that extreme, and I do not foresee myself turning into a woman.

I will not lie; the fact I needed this to mingle with these people made me disgusted and ashamed. Regardless of which world one'd inhabit, as long as someone differs from you in some way, it's nearly impossible to eradicate hatred.

Bias stems from an absence of knowledge of matters beyond one's scope of understanding.

I excused their behavior as resulting from ignorance, for they believed that they alone existed in their world, and outside of their city-states and Greece, there was nothing.

Many would have questions about the world surrounding them. With my capabilities, I would be apprehensive about regular humans. The truth is, I was not frightened of mortals. Rather, what filled me with dread was the group to which the Holy Warriors belong: the Tribunal!

Despite the amount of time and power I had, I was unable to locate their whereabouts. It was as if they had never existed to begin with.

By using Eternal Vigor, I transformed my appearance into that of a middle-aged man with blonde hair and blue eyes. My temporary skin was so pale that it looked as if it hadn't basked in sunlight for ages. Clad in a gray robe with a wooden cane in my grasp, I appeared every bit like the archetypal image of a mage or wizard.

My mind descended on Tiamat, the area under my control, and located a city-state that met my requirements. Teleporting there, I instantly materialized at the city's sparsely populated center.

It was impossible for me to know everything, but with the help of Tiamat and Acheron, it became apparent I could become all-knowing within the areas I controlled. Once they covered the world and even the universe, that is when I would have omniscience and omnipotence, one step away from rivaling God.

The darkness draped across the skies like a blanket. Scattered in the heavens were the moon and stars, shining with a wishful aura.

Torchlights illuminated every avenue as men and women thronged the roads, going about their business. Shuffling amidst the crowds were some men wearing distinct battle garments, conversing with their peers.

Welcome to Pylos City, a city-state that worshiped Poseidon, the god of the seas, above all else. There was something odd about this city. Despite the existence of gods, this city did not seem to be under their watchful gaze.

Ever since attaining my godhead, I have been able to vaguely sense the divine presence of some gods in some of the city-state temples. In Athens, there were actually two gods there, but even when I grew up under their noses, they did not attack, meaning that they were most likely sleeping.

Pylos City was situated adjacent to the Aegean Sea, providing a good location for communication and trade with lands situated across the sea.

Pylos and Cornith have been at odds for years over these trade routes, with Pylos always at a disadvantage.

I strolled through the city, endeavoring to immerse myself in the local culture and customs.

As I meandered through the city, I overheard a group of men at a nearby tavern gossiping. Their discussion revolved around the City Lord's reign and the bounty of their recent exploits at sea.

To my surprise, I discovered that the City Lord was fostering a cadre of soldiers-turned-pirates using the city's resources. The pirates would prey on ships that failed to remit their taxes, pillaging and looting their vessels.

This revelation brought to mind the Viking Age, an era steeped in legends of seafaring raiders and their occupation. However, since the Northern Highlands were divided by many races, where did the Vikings fit into this? Did they exist now, or is that something for the future?

In theory, if the Greek gods existed, it was likely that the Norse gods existed as well. I was not one to ignore this possibility. However, if that were so, the count of adversaries I would have encountered would have risen.

If the Greek gods were crazy, the Viking gods were even more dangerous. It was hard to say which one was weaker, but I'd have rather dealt with the Greek gods. Odin was not one to be trifled with. He possessed both power and wisdom, a bad combination to make an enemy out of.

Still, if the Greek gods' creation story was true, how would the Norse creation story come into play? Did these gods simply create their own part of the world, and that did all these creation stories collectively create Arctara? If that were so, it would be interesting.

I digressed.

Despite my limited stay, I have observed that, in terms of civic and cultural significance, Pylos seemed to outshine

Athens. What struck me most was the beaming faces of the locals, even as they toiled and perspired in their daily endeavors.

Sure, not everything was perfect. The city was deficient in many essential resources necessary to evolve into a formidable city-state. But there were things power could not achieve. Even with its strength, I have never seen anyone in Athens radiate so much gratitude and kindness. No one ever walked around with a smile on their face.

What struck me as confusing was that this was all happening in a city that worshiped Poseidon. It was odd, but I reminded myself that this was a different world, and there were bound to be some differences somewhere.

Pylos fit my requirements perfectly. Shutting my eyes, I used my connection with Tiamat to locate individuals with a latent talent for magic.

The speed at which the Weave spread was relatively slow, but unlike Tiamat and Archeron, which grew in tandem with my divine power, the Weave grew by absorbing energy from outside of Arctara and turning it into pure mana. The mana concentration might not be high here, but some people's bodies would still actively absorb it.

I felt my face scrunch in confusion after a couple of minutes. "Merely three? I was hoping to teach more than a hundred mages, but there were only three. If there are only three in Pylos, that would mean the total number of potential mages in all of the Northern Highlands is less than a hundred thousand!"

Although in a fantasy world, Mages were fewer in number than Knights, the number was still too low.

The requirements to become a mage weren't too high. Since becoming a Mage required connecting to the Weave, one's mind had to be strong enough to do so. However, if one couldn't hold mana in their bodies, the highest attainable level was Apprentice Mage.

To become an Official Mage, one had to be able to hold mana inside their body and create their own innate spells inside their mind-space.

Stepping forward, I instantaneously appeared inside an office lit with flickering torches.

The room appeared rather austere, with no embellishments or adornments of any kind.

Seated at the far end of the space and positioned directly opposite to the entrance was a fat man who appeared to be scowling as he sat behind his desk.

Adorning his desk were a carafe of crimson wine, succulent roasted fish served with a side of vegetables, and a pile of documents meticulously inscribed on yellow paper.

With a piece of fish crammed into his mouth and the other hand clutching a document, he momentarily set it down, scribbled something hastily, then picked up where he left off, alternating between the two with studied concentration.

It has been twenty years since he ascended to the esteemed position of City Lord, surpassing the accomplishments of even his illustrious father. However, he seemed to have finally encountered an equal adversary; despite his numerous and intricate strategies, he couldn't achieve any desirable outcomes.

If this was to continue, Pylos would become weaker and weaker in every generation!

PART 2: TEACHING

(Year 257, Month of the Leo)

"The Way of Magic is a dangerous path, if you are not careful, you could fall at any moment. No matter what rank you reach, it is important to remain cautious and choose your spells carefully." 'Jarth' cautioned, addressing his three attentive students.

In Pylos, aside from the City Lord Etna, there were two individuals who possess exceptional talents in magic: a young woman named Sophia, and a young merchant by the name of Teris.

"Over the last six months, we have gone over the basics of what it means to be a Mage. I have stopped you all from connecting to the Weave, so as to not have any regrets. Today, I will quiz you, whether you pass or not, you can decide if you want to connect to the Weave. Let's start with Sophia, can you tell me how many elements there are?" asked Jarth, looking at his brightest student with a smile.

Sophia was a petite blond girl with freckles on her face. She was a beauty. Her stunning green eyes shone with excitement as she answered her Teacher's question, "Teacher, there are five elements, Fire, Water, Wood, Metal and Earth. From these elements, many new ones are born."

With a smile and gratification, Jarth nodded. "That's correct. The world as we see it is essentially a combination of all these five elements. As you said, Sophia, when two elements combine, they can create an entirely new element. For instance, Wind and Water can create Ice. What this means is that, in theory, there are an infinite number of elements."

Turning his head, Jarth looked at the fat man, the City Lord of Plyos City. "Etna, could you enlighten us on the drawbacks of pursuing the way of magic?"

"Teacher, one of the glaring weaknesses of Mages is distance. If a warrior bridges the distance between us, we will be open and defenseless. So it is important for Mages to keep their distance and chant spells," explained Etna.

"You're correct. All Mages, no matter the rank, are weakest when casting a spell. A Warrior of the same rank is someone that must be kept at a distance. Generally, the stronger the Mage, the easier it is to react to sudden change. For example, an Official Mage can cause 0 Rank Spells or Apprentice spells without chanting, but Apprentice must chant spells because of their limited experience and knowledge of mana."

"Lastly, Teris, could you please shed some light on the hierarchy of mages?"

Teris, a young brown hair man with a innocent face and warm welcoming aura, replied, "The hierarchy of mages starts at Rank 0 Apprentice, followed by Rank 1 Official Mage, Rank 2 Grand Mage, Rank 3 Legendary Mage, and finally, the highest rank of Rank 4 Mythical Mage. Progressing through these ranks grants a mage a significant increase in power. A Mage of a higher rank can use lower level spells without much issue."

Jarth smiled at everyone and continued, "It seems like everyone has learned the basics. However, Teris, you need to remember, there is no end to the way of mages. As long as there is knowledge, then mages will continue to reach higher levels. The reason we became mages is to understand the world and learn everything there is. Do not limit yourself with thoughts of a limit, because once you do, you will only only be standing in your own way."

Teris bowed his head with acknowledgement.

Turning to look at his students, Jarth was pleased. He had spent a lot of time and effort to teach them his method of becoming Mages. There were a lot of altercation along the way but he, like them, has grown stronger in his knowledge.

"Everyone, you have reached the end of what I can teach you. Now you must go and acquire knowledge and grow as Mages."

"Sophia, assume the meditation pose and use your mind to connect to the Weave. Use the mana inside your body as a guide, follow it all the way to the limit."

"Yes, Teacher!" Exclaimed Sophia with excitement. She had been eagerly anticipating this moment for the past six months, and now she could possess the same power as her Teacher.

Sophia closed her eyes, and followed the method taught to her. It did not take long before she felt her mind flying upwards, reaching a vast and infinite world filled with countless spells.

In this world, there was a boundless tower, with many layers. Her mind was at the base of the tower, and could only see Rank 0 spells. Above the Rank 0 spells, she could vaguely make out spells of higher levels, which placed a small amount of pressure on her mind.

In the Rank 0 layer of the tower, the area looked chaotic with many different weather abnormalities happening at the same time. There was a blizzard in one corner, a volcano in the other. However, everything seemed to have an odd sense of order.

If one would look at the blizzard, one would see many ice spells scattered about. The deeper in they'd go, the stronger the spell would be. If one would reach the end, the spell might have had the strength of a weaker Rank 1 spell, despite being in the Rank 0 layer.

Sophia paused for a moment, taking in the view of all the mana that surrounded her. Then, she diligently began her search for the specific spell her instructor once mentioned, scanning through the multitude of spells until she found it.

Sophia was well aware that her first spell would have a significant impact on her development and the path she would take towards becoming an Official Mage. She approached her selection with great consideration and care, determined to choose the spell that best aligned with her goals.

Jarth had advised them about the importance of their apprentice spells, so no one dared to pick one at random. Whatever spell is chosen here, will influence what kind of Official Mage she will become in the future.

One of the advantages of picking good apprentice spells was the possibility of gaining an innate spell, which could be cast without fear of disappearing or incantation. These spells belonged to the user, not the Weave.

Mages with innate spells could create a Mage Family, as there was a chance of children being born with the innate spells. This would make things easier for them to become Mages.

Sophia did not have to think much about what type of spell to construct in her mindspace, as she already knew what spell she wanted. It was unorthodox to have it as a first spell but she did not have a choice.

In a world with deities, having this spell, if one was not a part of a clery, was bad news and one could easily become an enemy of the gods.

Minor Healing, was a spell that allows the user to heal anyone with healing magic. The greater the injury, the more mana and times they would have to cast the spell. But in this world, where not everyone could receive divine blessings from the gods, this spell was undoubtedly the best choice.

As long as she does not expose herself, there is no need to be worried about being hunted down.

Unlike her fellow apprentices, Sophia did not have the background to support herself to become an Official Mage.

While becoming an apprentice was easy, becoming an Official Mage required more resources and a lot of knowledge. Only with knowledge would one have the chance to become a true mage. If not, even an apprentice with some ideas could defeat an Official Mage.

Etna had shown a gesture as if he would be willing to take her in but Sophia was not stupid. Jarth had been blunt, explaining how cruel the world of mages was. It is not rare to find mages researching on people or doing sinister things. While she did not think this would happen now, the future was constantly moving, so it was unknown what changes Etna might grow through.

In the end, her and Etna's path did not align. She was not power hungry nor did she have a great ambition. Taking care of her siblings in the orphanage was already enough for her. As long as she takes care of them, she could smoothly advance on in way of mages.

As soon as she chose her spell, a strange power flowed into her body, and eventually her mind. Inside her mind, the spell model for Minor Healing was slowly forming, with the mana inside her body being the brush, and the mindspace the canvas.

She could feel her body brimming with lifeforce, making her curious about how long she could live for. Apart from her lifespan, there did not seem to be a physical change done to her body. She was still weak, even with the addition of the spell in her mind.

She thought perhaps once she condenses an offensive spell, she might experience some physical change.

This was not groundless,she had evidence to support her theory. Jarth was an Archmage, which was a Rank 3, Legendary Mage. Jarth was known as the Archmage of Fire, his body was close to the element of fire, it mightt as well be considered one.

His body was not simply flesh and blood anymore, but one close to being the element of fire. Probably even if you'd wound him, there would not be blood running out of his wound, but fire.

Examining her mindspace, Sohpia could see the spell model absorbing the mana inside her body to support itself and to increase its power.

Currently, her mindspace could only support one Rank 0 spell. Only when her mental strength grew could she condense a second one. But that was something that took time. If not because Jarth gave them the Soulfire Mediation Method, becoming an apprentice might have been an even harder task.

If everything was to go well, becoming an Official Mage in ten years was not impossible. This might have seemed long from a human point of view, but one had to remember that a mage's lifespan was far longer than a normal person.

The higher rank the Mage, the greater their lifespan. If a Mythical Mage's lifespan already rivaled that of a demigod, what about Mage above that?

It seemed unnecessary to think about that, since she has not even reached the first rank on the path of mages. Her current goal was to gain resources and transform her mindpace into a soul sea so she could become an Official Mage.

Only when one's mindspace becomes a soul sea can one create their own spell and be called an Official Mage. Technically an apprentice was not a mage since all they were doing is borrowing the spell from the Weave.

Although there was nothing wrong with that, if a Mage arrived in a dark zone, a place where the Weave was not present, would they still be called a Mage? Of course not. That is why an Official Mage had to create a soul sea, which was a smaller version of the Weave, and was always with them.

Even if they would enter a dark zone, they could still cast spells and wouldn't be defenseless.

As Sophia opened her eyes, a profound sense of exhilaration swept over her, and with immense gratitude, she bowed to her teacher. To become a Mage and wield otherworldly power was not something she very much thought about.

Most people were content with the simpler form of life and did not wish for much. However, that was because they did not know how many new things were out there for them to discover and experiment. .

Although thankful, Sophia was aware that she would be facing a lot of problems going forward. Jarth has not hidden anything from them. Some gods will not mind Mages but there were some out there who would definitely find ways to destroy them.

Although Jarth had said Mages had existed for a long time, Sophia was not stupid. If they really existed for such a long time, there would have been rumors or stories about them, but there was nothing.

Why did Jarth lie about this? She was not sure, but he had been good to her, so she did not want to think anything rude.

Etna and Teris sat down without any hesitation and entered into a deep meditative state, connecting with the Weave. Similar to Sophia, they had planned and contemplated what spell to choose. Their spells were ones that will aid them in their goals.

Unlike Sophia, they were not free and without concerns. Etna, for example, had many people who were out to kill him. If he'd chosen a spell like Sophia, it would be stupid.

Arriving inside the tower, Etna located the spell he was looking for in an area covered in darkness and fire. It seemed this spell had a connection to both elements.

The spell he chose was called Domination, a powerful Rank 0 Spell which might match some weaker Rank 1 spells in power.

Domination was quite distinctive in that, unlike most spells which vanish after use, it acted more like an innate ability, remaining dormant until enough mana energy was absorbed for further usage.

The spell Domination enabled the user to exert their will over the external world. With just their mental prowess, it's possible to suppress an individual or even to cause their demise. This spell was perfect for those with great ambitions.

Teris made an interesting and surprising selection, choosing the seemingly unremarkable Fireball, a spell many considered one of the weakest in the Rank 0 layer.

No one expected Teris to make this decision, so everyone was shocked when he did.

Jarth could comprehend the reasoning behind Etna and Sophia's spell choices. However, he found himself confused by Teris's choice. While it's said that power lies not with the spell itself but the user, there were other more powerful alternatives available, so why did he choose the seemingly inferior spell? While he pondered this, Jarth remained silent. After all, his obligation was to offer counsel and guidance, not to make decisions for them.

Jarth wasn't overly concerned about Teris. After all, as a wealthy merchant, he had ample resources and financial stability that would likely allow him to become an Official Mage at a rapid pace. As the wealthiest individual present, Teris possessed an advantage over his peers.

Jarth couldn't help but wonder if Teris's choice of the seemingly weak Fireball had been an attempt to mimic him. However, it was an exercise in futility, as Jarth was a true god and Teris was merely a mortal. He had no way of knowing whether the path he followed could lead him to achieve the status of a Grand Mage, let alone an official one.

Jarth secretly shook his head with a pleased smile as he congratulated the group. "It's been an honor to teach you all that I could. Where you go from here depends solely upon your perseverance and determination." He did not wait for them to say anything and simply disappeared in a ball of fire.

As Jarth arrived in the skies, he transformed back into Archeus.

Archeus couldn't help but smile with relief, pleased to see that his plan had gone better than expected. Not only had he succeeded in creating three budding seedlings of magic, but he had also deepened his understanding of his divine abilities in the process.

"Now, we are on the brink of the final step." Looking down at the three mages, he couldn't help thinking about Kaiser, wondering how things were going on his end.

Disappearing faster than when he vanished in the ball of fire, Archeus appeared somewhere else and waved his hand to reveal the entrance of a massive inverted mountain.

Inside this mountain's depths lay one hundred levels, each smaller than the one before. The biggest level was the first floor, which existed closest to the surface.

With another graceful hand gesture, Archeus conjured a small orb, infused with the elements of Yin and Wood. The orb pulsed with power and began to float out of his hand.

After the energy inside the orb reached its peak, Archues sent it into the mountain and watched as it fell through the floors until it reached its depths.

The mountain and the orb merged, resulting in tremors and the release of energy. The energy shook the surroundings, causing some wild animals to follow the energy and enter the mountain.

Archeus let out a pleased chuckle as he revealed his biggest accomplishment. "This is surprising; who would have thought some offhand remarks from my apprentice would allow me to create a Dungeon Core? Although its capabilities pale in comparison to those found in games, it has its own unique advantages and strengths."

Despite its limitations, the Dungeon Core possessed a remarkable ability. Although it could not create monsters from scratch, it boasted the power to transform any creature that entered it into its own monster. The monsters can become stronger by killing invaders or absorbing the energy used to create the Dungeon.

Of course, the Dungeon was not useless. If anyone were to defeat the monsters inside the Dungeon, they would have been embedded in energy, thus becoming powerful. Simply put, they would level up.

Compared to the path of Mages, Archeus was more interested in this new discovery. Compared to the Way of Mages, which would only affect a limited number of people, the Dungeon was more widespread and affected the entire world.

If he wanted to, he could create Dungeons all over, and the fantasy world he wanted would become closer to completion.

However, Archues was a bit hypocritical. He did not want to be an evil god, so just like Kaiser, he wanted someone to become the God of Madness and Evil. This god would be the god of monsters and dungeons.

CHAPTER 9

KING OF THE UNDERWORLD

(Year 254 of the Tribunal Calendar, Month of the Libra)

My name is Zexos, hailing from an era lost to the annals of history.

Once a mighty king of unparalleled power, I had everything that the world could offer, yet I wanted more. I conquered every wonder of the mortal world, but in my insatiable greed, I sought to conquer even death — and in the end, it was my undoing.

The power I held only caused me to descend into tyranny. I quelled opposition through force and seized what was not rightfully mine, until eventually, I found myself alone.

Those who once fought by my side now viewed me as a monster. Friends distanced themselves, lovers became nothing more than bones, and children remained forever trapped in their youth.

By the time I realized the extent of the devastation I had wrought, it was too late. Millions lay buried in their graves because of me. I am but a sinner, a butcher of men.

Sigh.

As death finally claimed me, I felt not the fury I had expected but only a sense of relief. No reason remained to cling to life; there was no one left to mourn my passing.

I thought I would be at peace once I died, but my journey was not over.

After my passing, I had the unfortunate opportunity to witness the events that unfolded after my death: my once-great empire lay fragmented, and the common people were finally fed. But my legacy was forever stained, and history would remember me only as the Bloody Butcher.

Despite the things I had left behind, my sins have overshadowed everything.

As a ghost, time held no sway over me, for I had conquered that which I most feared above all else: Death. However, I did not have the joy I had imagined. I was more empty than ever. What reason was there to conquer death if I had no one to enjoy it with?

There was no going back to right my wrongdoings; I could only walk deeper down this path of no return.

During my time as a ghost: I have come to understand that not everyone has the ability to become a ghost. Even for those who did, this existence offered only a brief reprieve from the inevitable.

There were two types of ghost, earthbound and free ghost. Earthbound are those who couldn't leave the place where they died. They were forever stuck, unable to explore the world they were in, even as ghosts.

Free ghosts were rare, and in my time, I have only discovered a few like me. A free ghost could leave their death sites and roam as they liked.

Roaming the mortal world like a specter of the night, I encountered many others who had lingered longer in this world than I had. Through their tales, I learned of hidden stories and secrets, for these spectral beings were more knowledgeable than the books I burned in my reign.

Through their tales, I came to understand the true vastness of this world; a place teeming with creatures and races beyond my wildest imagination. There were even lands where pyramids reached towards the skies, and across the sea was a realm of miniature people. Far to the south, warriors of darkness were said to roam.

Many things have changed since I was alive. It seemed that between the time I died and the time I awoke as a ghost, a vast amount of time had passed.

I was the only emperor in history to conquer the world; many have tried to emulate me but failed. However, despite my accomplishments, I was not honored or remembered. Even my sins were buried along with me.

Eons drifted by, and once again I found myself alone. The ghosts I had once met and befriended had long since faded into oblivion, unable to withstand the ravages of time. Yet I remained alone, for I was different somehow. Capable of enduring beyond the limits of mere existence.

Maybe, as a result of my heinous actions during my life, a malevolent energy now surrounds me. The souls of the millions I had ordered to their deaths were now under my command, and each year I drew upon the life force of one to sustain my own eternal existence. Thus, I should live for countless centuries to come, impervious to every known method of destruction.

Life and Death were just steps away, but the difference was like night and day.

In life, I was just a tyrant with absolute control over those I ruled. In death, I still ruled over those whom I had killed.

I could capture ghosts and have them join the area of darkness that followed me, but I did not do so. I never understood how I changed so much. I was a just ruler who loved my people but, over time, fell down a slippery slope, only to end up as a tyrant.

I ascended to the throne of the Sumerian Empire at the age of 9, after the passing of my father, Giligamash. I had loyal aides and a vast family to support me. In the beginning, I did right by them, but as the years passed on, fear of death began to haunt me.

I searched the world for the elixir of immortal life, but failed to find it. I tried many means, but death eluded me. Suddenly, I found a Shaman from a distant land who told me a way to live forever, which was killing people. As a result, I framed others for crimes they did not commit, and in my reign, more than a million souls were vanquished because of this belief.

Now, looking back, the Shaman did not lie, but this was not what I expected.

Sigh.

I do not remember how many times I appeared in the land of Greece during my travels, but this time, something felt different. The land was the same, and the people were the same; nothing was odd, but my intuition told me otherwise.

It was not long before I discovered the reason for the confusion.

A strange, omnipresent pull from an unseen power beckoned me forward into a world that seemed eager to embrace me and fulfill its intended purpose.

I did not resist and allowed the force to pull me in. With my current power over death, it was simple to resist since the power was not focused solely on me, but I did not. There was nothing else I found interesting in the mortal world; I had seen everything there was to see.

Accepting the call, I was violently hurled into a shadowy realm, a world I soon discovered was created by the Lord of Death, Adis.

In my days of roaming, I had not heard this name before. I heard of many gods and saw some by accident, but none of them could do what I witnessed.

The world was vast, with no end in sight. The land stretched as far as the eye could see. This land did not have the harmful rays of sunlight, but the cold power of the moon.

This place was the ideal place for beings like me, ghosts.

I was alone in this realm, and I could sense the towering aura of the Lord of Death. This strength was far greater than what I possessed.

As time went on, more and more ghosts appeared in the world, making it quite crowded.

After more than a thousand ghosts appeared, the Lord of Death explained the reason for the creation of this world, Archeron.

The arrival and departure of the Lord of Death were swift.

While this might not have been something significant for someone of Adis' caliber, I was thankful nonetheless. Many of my friends had indeed perished. Had this place existed before, perhaps I could see them once more.

Before Adis left, a palm-sized black rock descended from the skies, making many approaches to try their luck. However, despite it passing through many hands, the rock was left behind as no one could understand its purpose.

No one believed it was an ordinary rock; after all, Adis was the one who created it. It would be odd if it was.

Holding the rock in my hand, I immediately understood its powers. I was not sure why I knew, but I was surprised. The rock allowed control over the doors of Archeron. I could also appoint people to be in charge of Archeron's future.

If I utilized this rock correctly, I could regain rulership even in death, but I felt conflicted. I was once a ruler, but I was not a good one, so would it be smart to attempt again?

Could the experience I have guide me on the correct path?

After much contemplation, I decided to keep the rock. No one else seemed to understand the power the rock had, and it would be a waste to leave it. Plus, what reason did Adis have for leaving this rock here if not for someone to obtain it?

Finding a secluded location, I opened a door to the mortal world while walking outside. Even though the sun was up, I did not feel it doing any harm to my body. The rock completely protected me from any harmful things that could happen to me.

Though this was amazing, it didn't make me feel many emotions. I could already endure the rays of the sun. Even if it were to harm me, the millions of souls I have under my command would die in my place, keeping me safe.

After thinking for a moment, I decided to return to Archeron and put some order in place.

At this moment, Archeron was a world of scattered sand without a firm hand to lead.

CHAPTER **10**

DAWN OF A NEW WORLD

Throughout Greece and the surrounding areas, shocking pieces of information traveled like wildfire. The Village of Crista, a small village settlement near Athens, was ruthlessly massacred, leaving no survivors!

No one could believe this at first, but as it spread, they had no choice but to accept it as the truth. No one could understand who was behind it. Who had the courage to stroke the hair of Athens? Were they not afraid of the Athenian Guards?

While it had been a long time since the Athenian Guards had moved, that did not mean they were weak. They possess one of the strongest military forces in Greece, not something many could dare to threaten.

It had taken a couple of days for Athens to realize something had happened in Crista, as the regular drop-off of corps deadlines had been missed. This raised suspicion from those in charge.

Of the many villages around, Crista had a special place in the hearts of Athenians, as it is a village as old as Athens, named by the goddess herself.

Unlike the other villages which required guards to go and inspect things, Crista only needed to bring a specific amount of food at a set time. They have never missed this deadline in their long history, so unless something happened, the Oligarchs did not believe Crista would fail to show up.

With this in mind, the Oligarchs sent a group of soldiers to investigate, hoping it was nothing serious. Sadly, they were too optimistic.

When the guards arrived at the location, they could not help but vomit and tremble with shock and fear. The scene was like something from a nightmare!

Limbs and blood were scattered everywhere. Mangled corpses littered the ground. Women and children were violated, and their clothes were violently ripped apart.

This could have only been the work of demons, as no human would have ever committed such a monstrous act.

The guards did not stay around a moment longer and immediately reported to their superiors.

The top management of the city, after hearing the reports, placed a gag order on the incident, but how could paper conceal fire? It was unknown if it was the guards or someone else, but the information spread like wildfire.

On the streets alone, everyone was talking about the incident. It was not everyday that something like this happened, with no idea of who was responsible.

Some people were able to figure it out and did not dare to continue anymore.

Another incident reached many ears when an escort troupe, while escorting merchants, discovered a place where monsters from legend resided. Killing the creature would grant you strength and yield numerous peculiar items within.

When this information spread, many warriors flocked to the location to test their luck and become stronger in the process, spreading the news further.

The tide of the world was changing in an unknown direction.

(Unknown Location)

"Who is spreading this news? We must find them and have them executed!" An old man in a black robe with a strange cane in his hand said as he slammed his cane into the ground angrily.

A young girl in white robes and a priest's hat said indifferently, "It is obvious that someone with ulterior motives is doing this. No one knew we were the ones behind the Crista incident. Even if they did, would they dare to spread it?"

Another person, fully cloaked, spoke in a hoarse tone, "We must figure everything out something fast. The Tribunal must not come to light."

"..."

Things were getting out of control. After they dealt with the situation in one location, something else happened elsewhere. Unlike before, the gods did not notice the situation until the escorts reported it.

The old man sat down, feeling frustrated. From the establishment of the Tribunal until now, no one has been able to escape the eyes of the gods. Even if it was a god from the outside world, as soon as they entered a place influenced by the gods, they would be spotted.

All gods needed faith, so the creation of that unknown place was not something they could understand. The faith of the gods has not lessened, meaning it was not a god's doing. But there were no records of something similar happening in the past.

"Have we sent people to observe?" The young girl asked.

The cloaked man answered with tiredness in his voice, "Unfortunately, if we send people, it might cause problems. Many people are flocking to the area, and it's not impossible for other organizations to show up as well."

If it were normal, they would have sent some members to eliminate the problem, but they couldn't. There were no signs of a god, nor were there signs of the collapse of faith. The gods have taken a wait-and-see approach.

"The situation is not good for us either. Only a few of the gods are awake right now, which means our means are limited," the girl said.

"That's not good. Before, we only had Zeus, Hades, Apollo, and Athena awake, so who fell asleep now?"

"Zeus."

The three were silent. There was never a time that Zeus fell asleep, so why did he do it now? Could he not see things going in an unknown direction?

After the incident with Poseidon, the gods tactfully decided to take turns staying awake to observe the world, but as time went on, the faith the gods received was becoming less and less, making it difficult for them to stay awake.

Zeus' faith, while weakened, has not reached the stage of falling asleep. As the Chief God of the Greek pantheon, there were not many city-states that did not worship him. So in the eyes of the three, this was strange.

Their eyes flickered as they looked at each other, many thoughts running through their minds. At some point, they seemed to have come to the same conclusion, worrying that what had happened to Poseiden would happen again.

Just like Zeus, Poseidon, and Hades were the three pillars of the Greek pantheon. Even if people stopped believing in other gods, this was unlikely to happen to them.

In the past, some unknown person had found a way to stop faith from reaching Poseidon, which caused him to fall into a deep state of sleep. While he has not fallen, he might as well have, since he had not made an appearance in more than a thousand years.

With the absence of this powerful god, the world descended into chaos, with a world- ending catastrophe shaking the world. The entire world was flooded without the god of the seas to calm it.

The old man asked the young girl, "Did Zeus leave any words before he went to sleep?"

The girl shook her head and said, "No. Father had only said this might not be a bad thing in regards to the monster situation. If we utilize it properly, we can create new faith in the gods and have them awake once more."

True. The gods had nothing to lose, but much to gain. Instead of destroying the mountain, it was best to encourage more people to go there. To say they were not interested in going as well would have been a lie.

After all, according to the information they got, as long as one defeats the monsters, one could increase one's strength. They have been at the limit of the demigod stage for many years. If not for the fact that it was difficult to ignite the divine flame without followers, all three of them would have become gods long ago.

However, since the playing field had already been established, it was difficult to squeeze into the divine stage without offending some god.

Greece and Rome were the core of faith for the gods, but the situation in Rome was not looking good. They have been encouraging the belief in the one true god for many years and even though they have worked hard to counter it, it was not easy to change people's beliefs.

Now, the pantheon of gods could barely survive on the faith of the Greek people. If that was affected, the gods could fall, which would be disastrous. But it might not be bad for them. After all, as long as they could replace the gods, the damage done to the world would be prevented, but that was harder said than done.

"What about the 'Lord'? We gave him a couple of days to do what he must because of the divine heart he gave us. Should we do something about him?"

The 'Lord' is a demigod from Persia, an enemy nation.

Unlike Greece, which has been weakened in the current age, Persia was a massive empire beyond the seas. Even Rome and Greece, combined, could not match their strength. Because, unlike their counterparts, Persia has been tightened with one belief system, making the gods there vastly stronger.

"There is no need to worry about him. He wouldn't dare to linger longer than he had to. Although their Chief God is powerful and is not to be taken lightly, he is a benevolent god and would not make things difficult for us."

Ahura Mazda was a reclusive god who rarely showed up, but even if one might not have been friendly to Persia, everyone was clear about his conduct. He was truly fitting of the title 'Supreme Lord'.

"The thing he must have lost must have been pretty important if he was willing to give us one of his divine hearts. It's just a pity he gave us the useless one."

A divine heart was the core of a god's power. When one reaches the limit of the demigod stage, it is possible to condense it. If someone were to fuse with it, they would be able to become a demigod in one step but forever incapable of progressing further. After all, the heart did not belong to them.

"'Divine Heart of the Crimson Moon' is not bad. If I could absorb it, I would reach another step, but it conflicts with my path."

Fusing with a divine heart that conflicted with one's path was not a smart choice. If it was compatible, it could increase the strength of one divine heart, pushing them closer to the realm of God.

"I hear he is one of the few demigods who is able to walk more than one path simultaneously. If we could figure this out, even if we don't become gods, we might be closer to their power."

A person could only have one divine heart inside their body. If they had more than one, they would not be able to withstand the power and would explode. The 'Lord' being able to do so must have been due to the Supreme Lord's care.

"So do we agree to wait and see?"

The cloaked man nodded. "Agreed."

"I think we should send someone to gauge the situation, but I agree," the petite girl added.

The old man agreed with the girl.

(Year 257: Month of the Scorpion, the Three Stars came to a consensus.)

CHAPTER 11

FIRST CONTACT WITH THE GODS

(Year 257 of the Tribunal Calendar, Month of the Taurus)

Observing everything from Tiamat, Archeus couldn't hide his smile, feeling relieved. He was scared that the Tribunal would interfere with the Dungeon, but so far he had not noticed anything out of place. In fact, many people were going to the Dungeon.

Even though he didn't feel good not knowing much about his enemy, a part of him was glad that they hadn't shown up to mess with his plans. But in case they appeared, he had a plan: he was going to follow them and locate their headquarters. That would have been the first step in getting to know his foe better.

The first mages were created. Now, all he had to do was wait for his three students to spread the magic to more people. He wasn't worried about this not playing out as he had imagined. Out of his three students, he had the highest hopes for Sophia - once she would grow as a mage, everything would fall into place by itself.

Sophia was the most kind-hearted one out of them, which is why he did not hesitate to teach her more than he taught the others.

Once the Dungeon and magic were more widespread, it would not be long before he could see a clear picture of Warriors and Mages fighting.

Inside his room, Archeus lay on his bed, his mind observing everything under his sphere of control.

Everything was going well inside Archeon. Ghosts were being drawn to it. Compared to the beginning, there were perhaps more than a million ghosts inside. Thankfully, since he became a god, Tiamat and Acheron have increased in size, and they are still growing, slowly but unmistakably.

Archeus' attention was grabbed by the ghost, who took his rock and was able to use it. He created the rock as a test to see if a ghost would be able to use it, and seeing it unwind in front of his eyes made him proud of his own intelligence.

There was no doubt that Archeus was a genius, and he was using his brain and power to create a world better than the ones he already knew; he was sure of it.

Perhaps the only reason the rock functioned as it did was because of Archeron. Being in his domain and given the ability to the rock, it makes sense it would work. Even if the ghost goes to Arctara, as long as he stays within the coverage of Tiamat, it will function. However, if it leaves the coverage of either Archeron or Tiamat, it might no longer function and would be a regular rock.

Archeus did not mind the ghost ruling over Archeron. That was the reason he created the rock in the first place. They needed to be able to function properly and become a powerful realm rivaling Tiamat.

He wanted to create a reincarnation cycle, but he was not sure how to do it. Plus, it did not make sense for him to do everything by himself. If he were to do everything on his own, then creating a fantasy world would have no point whatsoever.

He was only responsible for creating the base of it, and the rest was for the creatures living in his fantasy world to create.

It was a pity that he did not know what method to use to make the ghost more powerful. Creating a functional realm for the dead was already a miracle. It would be wrong to assume he could do literally everything he could think of.

However, there was something strange about this ghost that made him powerful enough as it was. Far more than what he expected. Compared to all the ghosts Archeus was looking at, this one might have as well been the king amongst them. The ominous cloud of darkness that followed him around was odd, but it made him look intimidating.

He truly appeared to be the King of the Underworld.

Tiamat looked the same as the last time he checked on it, apart from becoming bigger. It was not different from the mortal world, if we ignore the fact about how barren and lifeless it seemed.

Archeus did not try to do anything with it, mainly because he was not sure what to do. Perhaps in the future, he would get some ideas, but as of now, he doesn't have any.

As for Maria? She had become engrossed in her world. Although their relationship has not worsened, they have become somewhat distant. They hadn't spoken since the argument about his changing ways.

Archeus had no idea what to do about it. It was not what he expected their relationship to be.

His thoughts were suddenly interrupted, and his eyes snapped open, before he teleported somewhere in Greece.

Archeus was face-to-face with a beautiful woman wearing a golden dress made of armor with a bow and arrow on her back. The armor had some unique inscriptions that he imagined were runes. Her golden hair flowed without wind, and her blue eyes were calm without ripples.

In her hand, she was holding a golden shield with the medusa's head carved into it. At her waist was a slender sword that had a cold edge. Even when light touched it, it seemed to split in half.

She looked like a battle maiden, ready to enter the war. She looked so beautiful that every other woman paled in her comparison. Her clear skin shone with golden light, making her look like a porcelain doll.

Archeus had no doubt this was a goddess, a true one!

The calm voice of the goddess reached his ears, sounding soothing and intoxicating. "I thought it was finally time we met each other, don't you think, foreigner?"

"It is an honor to meet face-to-face, but I am sure you did not decide to signal your location like this just to see me." While he might have been surprised by her appearance, there was one thing he for sure wasn't, and that's dumb. He already knew this would happen sooner or later. The gods were aware of his existence; it was already a surprise that he could reach his current stage without them interfering.

While this was under the guise of them not being real, he was thankful. If he were aware they existed, he would not have done some of the things he had done, but things have reached this stage, and he is not afraid anymore.

Unless the entire pantheon of Greece attacked him, Archeus did not see himself dying. He was confident in his immortality. Although he was not an opponent to the twelve main gods, he could easily escape if he wanted to.

"True, I have my reasons to call you here." The goddess descended from the skies to the ground, retracting all the otherworldly aura around her. Now, she did not look any different from a mortal, but her power was still there.

Archeus could not gauge how powerful she was, but he could feel some pressure from her, meaning she was probably stronger than him.

Arriving next to her and retracting his power, Archeus observed her carefully while also keeping an eye on his surroundings. He had been cautious from the beginning, making sure this was not an ambush. He was not sure if the gods could escape his detection, but since they were gods, he had to be careful.

If the gods were able to locate him without him even being aware of it, thinking the gods could not hide their presence from his eyes was foolish.

When his realms expanded, he could sense the presence of the gods in some secret locations, but he was not sure if this was done intentionally because they sensed his presence or not.

Looking at the black man with calm eyes standing in front of her, the goddess spoke, "My name is Athena, the Goddess of War and Wisdom. Should I call you the God of Wishes, Kris, or something else?"

Archeus smiled wryly. He was not surprised she knew his epithet, which the mortals in Critas called him, but it was embarrassing to hear that from the mouth of a real god. However, since he decided to walk this path, embarrassment was something he had to toss aside.

"You can simply call me Archeus, the God of Omnipotence."

Athena looked at Archeus with surprise for the first time and nodded, seemingly not minding the obscurity of the situation. Even her father did not dare to claim omnipotence, but from what she had witnessed so far, she did not think it was unfounded.

Creating an Underworld and another realm was truly amazing. Even her uncle, Hades, was quite amazed by it. If not for the situation, perhaps Hades would have descended and spoken with Archeus himself.

After all, the Underworld was broken and could not function properly anymore. Although this affected her uncle, he was not the god of the underworld, so he did not fall asleep.

"There are a few reasons why I called you here, but first, let me ask you: what is your intention towards

Greece? We have been observing you, and we noticed you created a temple in Crista. Are you attempting to steal faith from us?"

Archeus frowned. "Faith is something you gods need; I can survive without it. I was attempting to test a theory of mine, and I got my answers. Since you are asking me something, let me ask you this: Why did you allow the Tribunal to slaughter the villagers? Does that not compromise your so-called faith?"

Athena was silent and looked at Archeus for a moment before answering, "Odd, I thought since you called yourself a god, you would understand, but it seems you are still clinging to being a mortal."

Looking into the skies with thoughts flickering in her mind, Athena answered, "Faith, as you said, is something we need in order to survive. Without it, we will fall asleep, as the best- case scenario, or die, as the worst-case scenario. Although, as long as people still believe in us, we will never truly die. The Tribunal's action was not my doing; it was something some of the gods decided on. I am sure you are aware, but Crista is named after my youngest daughter. Though not my blood child, she was one of my most devoted priestesses. I wanted to honor her, so I allowed the creation of the Village. The others deemed your approach to be a problem, and the situation happened as you said."

Archeus sighed, knowing that she wasn't lying to him; she had no reason to keep the truth from him. In the end, the Villagers died because of him, and that was something he couldn't deny.

Athena's gorgeous face contorted as she looked at Archeus with slight anger. "Although it happened, it was not without benefit. Because of you, souls with no place to go can move on. Still, I try to be rational, but I cannot. Why did you bring such a disaster close to Athens?! If it wasn't for my father, I would have punished you!"

Archeus did not know what to say. How was he supposed to tell her he did not foresee an incident happening? Even if there was a reason, he doubted she would be happy with his answer; after all, many died because of his incompetence.

He had attempted to rewind time to the point before the incident, but even with all his divine power, controlling time was not something he could use rashly. Just to go back a second, his divine power was gone in the mud, without even a ripple to show for it.

Sighing and shaking her head, Athena looked into the skies again, pondering.

"You have caused great damage to Crista and those in Athens; I think this is worth a favor for me to ignore, don't you think?"

What could Archeus possibly say to that? Of course, he had to agree. Although he saw the gods as his enemies, if he could have a friend or an ally amongst them, he would be a fool to refuse it.

Satisfied with his promise, Athena smiled at him. "Thank you. My next question is about your plans. You have given that mortal a part of your power; what is your end goal there?"

Kaiser? Archeus was not sure if he should tell her his plans, but he figured it would become obvious in the future, so why wouldn't he?

"My plan does not bring any harm to you or the other gods; instead, it brings benefits. Think about it; why do you think the faith in the gods has lessened?"

Athena pondered, but shook her head. Had she known the answer, they could have resolved the problem much earlier, avoiding their current predicament.

"It's because mortals are no longer dependent on the gods. As time goes on, eventually the gods will become mere myths and legends told to children but not taken seriously. I am trying to stop this by making this world stay in its current state. However, if I do this without finding a replacement for what they would have achieved on their own, my plans would fail."

"So you are saying…" Athena's eyes were shining with curiosity.

Archeus did not answer her question; instead, he continued, "If we work together, the gods will not only become more powerful; it will make you an important part of their lives. By changing the world and allowing them access to the power you gods limit, this world will become more colorful."

Athena did not say anything, thinking about the pros and cons. The more she thought about it, the more feasible the idea became. She was surprised that a simple mortal turned god could think of this. Even she, worshipped for her intelligence, couldn't come up with something like this.

Reaching out her beautiful hand, Athena felt a mysterious power permeating the air and grabbed it.

It was quite interesting; it was like divine power but far weaker. Indeed, even if the mortals possess this power, they could never be a match for the gods. She kept wondering about his thought process.

Archeus looked surprised as Athena played with the mana in her surroundings. The gods truly were unfathomable. Even he could not command mana in the same manner, despite knowing more about it.

Maybe Maria wasn't as proficient with her ability as she thought she was.

"You called this power mana. It is quite unique. Explain your plans a bit more; how would mortals who harness this power give us faith?"

Archeus was not surprised; she knew what mana was. While he has learned how to mask his presence from the gods, the same cannot be said about his apprentices. If the gods truly wanted to, they could nip them in the bud, before the mages could grow.

It was not like he was trying to hide this from anyone, but it was interesting to see how involved the gods were in this world. Even in Olympus, the gods have not taken their eyes away, despite the fact that they are becoming weaker.

"My plan is that when a Mage casts a spell, they must speak the name of a god, thus indirectly providing faith. For example, to use fire spells, they could recite Hephaestus' divine name, granting him faith, and the Mages the power to cast the spell. However, this is only for weaker Mages, once they reach a higher rank, they will no longer have to recite spells. But I do not think this is a problem. There will be more lower-ranking Mages than higher-ranking ones. What do you think?"

Athena found the plan good. It was like killing two birds with one stone. If the others found out about this plan, they would definitely be on board. However, not everyone would be able to be so open-minded. There are bound to be those who disagree. After all, why would they have to work with a mortal?

Though Athena did not care that Archeus was not a god in the proper sense, he did have the power to challenge some weaker ones. Because of that, she did not consider him a mortal but someone of equal standing with her.

"So, in conclusion, you do not intend to become our enemy? And instead plan to help us?" Athena asked.

"If I don't have to be one, I don't see a reason for us to be enemies. If you guys exist, it will make my world more colorful."

She nodded in agreement. "I do not have any more questions. I will talk to the others about this and see what they decide."

Archeus felt a relief wash over his entire body. Although he did not care if they were on board, he knew that having them by his side would make things easier.

Athena returned to her true form, filling the area with divine radiance, and was about to leave when Archeus stepped in front of her, causing her divine face to frown slightly. "Is there something else?"

"No, I was wondering if we could meet again. I created a world. I plan to host the gods in the future. If you do not mind, maybe…"

How could the wisest of the gods not realize what he was thinking? Even though he brought up some excuse, his eyes couldn't hide his thoughts.

Athena could see that Archeus was interested in her, but she chose to remain chaste because gods are not loyal or able to control their desires. If not because she did not see any lustful thoughts in his eyes, she would fight him here and now.

She has been chaste for so long, so she did not understand many things. She has thought of having a partner before, but no one has ever met her requirements. Archeus was quite smart and did not seem to be one to be lustful, and he had great control. Despite having great power, he did not cross many lines, and when he did, he made sure to right his own wrongs.

Athena did not mind his appearance, as she had lived a long time and seen many things. If anything, his appearance was quite attractive to her.

Pondering, she decided to give it a go. She knew the others would be shocked, especially those who had chased her for a long time, but she did not mind. What was the point of living forever without love?

"We will meet again." Taking a piece of her armor off, Athena gave it to Archeus and left in a flash of golden light.

Holding the warm piece of metal in his hand, Archeus smiled. He could still smell the fragrance of Athena on it, making him feel weak inside.

Giving someone something precious is a sign of courtship in Greece. He did not expect the gods to also have this tradition.

From the moment he saw Athena, he was already taken back. She was so beautiful and sophisticated. While beauty was not something he focused on, she matched everything he wanted in a woman; she was calm and collected.

Creating a pocket dimension, Archeus gently placed it inside and returned to Tiamat with a smile on his face. To show how happy he was, all the flowers in the realm bloomed at the same time.

Maria was inside her room, with books scattered across her desk. She had seen everything that happened and was happy for her son.

The moment Athena manipulated mana, Maria felt it, and her will descended. Although she did not focus on the conversation, she could tell with just a glance that Archeus was in love.

Looking at the documents on her desk, she sighed with depression. Even after so much time, she did not figure out how to change the world the way she wanted to, but it was not without result.

"In the end, I also change. Freedom is such an illusionary concept. To give one freedom is to take it from others. Only in death can there be true freedom. No matter how powerful one is, this is something they cannot escape. If I want to create a world where people are happy, I can only make them the masters of their own fates."

If Archeus were here, he would be surprised to see that in the documents Maria had written on, there is a rudimentary form of a reincarnation cycle! As long as it was followed, it was impossible for the reincarnation system to bloom.

CHAPTER **12**

THE SITUATION OF
THE DARK ELF

(Location Unknown)
(Year 257 of the Tribunal Calendar, Month of the Scorpion)

Deep inside a mountain, hidden from view, numerous small huts dotted the landscape. In the middle of the night, gathered around a campfire, some figures were roasting a white boar over the open fire, laughing with one another.

The atmosphere was just right; the pale shape of the moon hung overhead, and the darkness of the night consumed the land. The fireplace seemed to be the only source of light within miles of the location.

The flickering fire cast long, worn shadows on the ground, yet it couldn't mask the peaceful undertone.

Sitting on a log with his family and a few other women, Kaiser looked into the dancing flames, his emotions hidden in his eyes. Looking at his wife and daughter's smiling faces, he could not help but feel overwhelmed with happiness. However, he wasn't able to get rid of the memories of that day that were haunting him.

Around this time of year, the village would usually have a celebration in honor of Athena and the other gods. There would be many people getting dressed in their best clothes and walking around with their friends, but no one brought it up today.

He could not blame them. While there were many great memories there, a shadow was cast over their lives. He was happy to see his wife and daughter again. Following the guidance of the God of Wishes, Kris, it did not take long before he found them.

They were exhausted and stricken with fear of what just transpired. The memories were fresh. Even he was scared and worried that the people who slaughtered the village would decide to track them down.

Finding them in that hollow state, Kaiser did everything he could to calm them down and reassure them, but to no avail. His change in appearance did not make things easier. He had to console them and bring up memories to make sure they knew it was him.

He was now a tall, handsome man with pale white skin and white hair. His eyes shone with a hue of redness, as if forever in the state of weeping. His missing arm was now attached, and he possessed hidden powers.

It was not odd that they had doubts if it was him; even he would have doubted them if they accepted him, simply for his word.

After reuniting with his wife, Kaiser told her his plans of finding somewhere secluded to live since if they'd go somewhere else, they would not be far from capture.

To be able to kill everyone in the village without cause or reason, those people had to have a considerable amount of power. Their organization was good and their strength was far superior to those of Sparta, which was not good news but it was a good method to gauge the enemies strength.

Kaiser vaguely remembered when the people attacked; they shouted 'heretics' and 'false gods', so he thought he had an idea of what they were there for. It would make sense why Kris would not hesitate to give him the opportunity to become a god.

He did not believe everything Kris said; however, he had no choice at the time but to accept what Kris was offering. Kaiser knew that if he had refused, he would have never seen his family again. The chances of him surviving that day were too small to gamble with his life.

Looking down at his hands, Kaiser could feel the power coursing through his veins, but he was not happy to feel it. This power came at a high price, so many lives with memories attached to them.

He imagined that if he did not know them, the pain he was feeling would not have been this great.

Today marked the third year they have been in these mountains, which have become their safe haven. It was well protected, making it easy for them to escape from pursuers.

Remembering the events that transpired on the way here, Kaiser could not help but look at the four women and two men sitting across from him with a hint of solemnity.

Unlike his family and the rest, Kaiser was someone who was once in the Athenian military; he had high rank and earned a lot of money, which was why he could afford to have such a huge house within Crista.

He was raised by his father, who taught him the way of warriors. He used those skills to climb the ladder and befriend quite a few nobles. While he was not influential by any means of the word, he was quite well known.

Kaiser had chosen to leave after he got married and was expecting a child, but he wondered if that was the correct choice. If he had stayed, perhaps his family would not have had to carry this heavy weight on their shoulders, but the fickleness of fate was something he couldn't predict.

Maybe even if he did stay, something else would have happened that would have led him down the same path.

These people were driven by desperate circumstances and had no choice but to leave their homes and wander around. From their words, it was not hard to see war on the horizon.

Argoes was planning to go to war with Corinth. If that happens, many people will suffer, mainly the common people. For them to travel this far by foot, it could be seen how dangerous the situation has become.

However, the years in the mountains moved on without much to show for it. They were cut off from the outside world; it was difficult to say how much the world had changed in that time.

He did have his reasons for allowing these people to come with him. Unlike him, his family was not able to support themselves in the mountains. It made sense to bring people along. However, he had to kill quite a few suspicious ones.

He would not allow them to get anywhere near his family. They already suffered enough, and he did not plan to allow anything bad to happen ever again to them.

These people could keep his wife and daughter company while helping around. However, his concern was mostly for the women.

He did not forget the task given to him by Kris. Eventually, he would have to pay for it, but right now, he was limited in the things he could do. He had to produce more offspring to make sure his race didn't fade out. Only with more of his kind could he become a god, but it was hard to bring the topic up with his wife.

He did not want to be in a relationship with anyone else, as he only loved his wife. But the circumstances warranted a more direct approach.

Looking down at his daughter sleeping on his lap, Kaiser felt joy in his heart. Running his fingers through her pure brown hair, he could not understand why anyone would try to harm her. She has witnessed things no child should have seen but did not show it.

This pained him greatly. He wished he could have been a better father, but it was impossible to change the past now. He has been living in peace for so long that thoughts of fighting rarely crossed his mind. Weakness was truly the ultimate sin. If he had been prepared, would things have happened the way that they did?

Glancing from the corner of his eye, Kaiser saw his wife, a beautiful young woman with long brown hair, green eyes, and pale white skin. She truly was the most beautiful woman he ever saw.

He remembered when he was courting her how hard it was to make her fall in love with him, but from then on, every single day they had spent together has been fulfilling.

Holding her hand, Kaiser could feel her tensing up slightly, but soon she calmed down. Even after so much time has passed, she still has not recovered from what happened to her.

Looking at her bulging belly, he smiled a little, knowing Emila would not be alone anymore.

Kissing her on the cheek, Kaiser whispered as if not to wake Emila, "Darling, do not worry; I am here. I promise that will never happen again."

Diana nodded and leaned her head on Kaiser's shoulder. "I am not worried. I still have the memories and the recurring nightmares, but I am relieved that we all get to be here together as a family. I do not blame you; you did everything you could, even going as far as risking your life for us. I cannot thank you enough for that."

Kaiser simply kissed her forehead and let the silence linger on.

After a moment, Diana broke the silence and said, "I think you should accept them. Those women will make us stronger. I am not worried about you falling in love with them; I know you."

Kaiser felt his shoulder become light and saw that his wife was now staring into his eyes. There was no anger or regret in her voice, but an odd sense of relief.

Looking into those eyes and staring back at him, Kaiser felt a sense of guilt. He would have brought this up later, but to have her say this to him made him feel ashamed.

There were many people with multiple wives in the village, but he did not believe love could be split among so many people. Favoritism and many other factors would eventually cause problems down the line.

Diana had wanted him to get more wives as it would increase his image, but he refused to do so. However, today, the same thing was said, and this time he didn't say no.

Kaiser did not tell Diana everything that happened in the temple or about his agreement with Kris. Not because he did not trust her, but because she would not understand. What he did tell her was how he had to reproduce and have many children. Unfortunately, despite trying it over the years, she has only now managed to get pregnant.

The reproduction of elves was not high, as stated by that mysterious voice.

"I am sorry, Diana; I truly am. I do not have another in this heart of mine but you and our family. Even if someone else carries my children, that will not change."

Diana smiled. "I know. Compared to the men I have seen, you are a gem that can only be seen by me. If many were like you, perhaps things would be different."

Diana once again rested her head on Kasier's shoulder, closing her eyes with tears flowing down her cheeks.

He did not know what to do. Even though she agreed, it was obviously something she wasn't happy about. Sadly, this was something good for him, and he couldn't take a step back.

Turning his gaze to the flames, Kaiser noticed the four women were looking at him, but they quickly turned away once their eyes met his. They probably overheard the conversation, but it would have happened sooner or later anyway, so he did not mind.

The two men did not seem concerned or worried that the women were all taken by Kaiser. To them, as long as they had food and a place to stay, everything was worth it. Compared to escaping the flames of war, women were nothing. Even though they saw firsthand how powerful Kaiser was, they would have responded the same even if they hadn't witnessed it with their own eyes.

Looking at the boar, the previous sense of hunger seemed to have disappeared.

CHAPTER 13

COHESION

Under the cover of night, dark ghostly figures could be seen chasing after other ghostly figures through the woods at high speed.

They moved so fast that the figures flickered from place to place without affecting anything in their surroundings. There was no disturbance, no wind, and no footsteps, yet the figures moved silently.

After rushing for a few moments, three ghostly figures appeared together in an opening, dressed from head to toe in dark robes that had a white eagle extending its talons downwards to capture its prey on their chest. In their hands, they were holding a long black chain that could be seen extending in the distance without touching the ground. On their backs, a black scythe rested, gleaming under the moonlight.

With their clothing choices, the three looked like Grim Reapers out to claim souls. And what's amusing is that this was precisely their action.

The leader of the group, a dark figure with a white band around his right arm, said, "He is a slippery one. It's unbelievable that he managed to slip away from us. It does not make sense. We have chased him quite a distance, yet he is considered an Earthbound ghost?"

Everyone knew that an Earthbound ghost couldn't leave the area they died in. In their time as Ghost Catchers, they have only come across a few free ghosts because of how rare they were. Unlike Earthbounds, who were tied to a location because of immense resentment, free ghosts had no resentment or longing and thus were free to wander as they pleased.

The others shook their heads. This did not align with the information they received in training.

"The information we got was most likely wrong."

The other Ghost Catcher spoke with some reverence in his voice, "Maybe the Ghost King could help us. However, we are little Ghost Catchers; it's possible that he won't even see us."

The leader listened to his subordinates' words but did not refute them. There were many cases of this happening throughout Archeron; the higher-ups were probably already figuring out a solution.

The system of Archeron has just been created, and many flaws are emerging. Such things take time to fix. It was already good to have such a seamless system in place in such a short amount of time; it would be selfish to request further adjustments when they knew it was still being developed. It was only a matter of time before it would become flawless.

Looking up at the skies, the leader noticed the moon had disappeared at some point, with the rays of sunlight creeping up from the distance. "We have been out here for too long; let's go back."

The leader pulled out an item from his cloak and crushed it, causing a dark portal to appear. All three of them stepped into the portal and disappeared.

Not long after they left, the ghost returned to the area, breathing a sigh of relief. Although he escaped from those strange ghosts, he almost got caught a few times, and that made him quite cautious of them.

He was not sure where those ghosts came from, but as soon as they saw him, they shouted about returning to the Underworld and sought to capture him.

He had heard of some ghosts vanishing from the surrounding areas, making him wary of things in the surrounding area. Thankfully, he was prepared; otherwise, who knows what they would have done to him?

Walking outside the portal, the three Ghost Catchers appeared in a city square filled with many other Ghost Catchers, coming and going on missions.

If someone was not familiar with this scene, they would be shocked to witness it, but this was a normal day in Archeron.

Unlike the orderless realm it used to be, many ghosts were able to make a living doing jobs and becoming ghost officials. This was all thanks to the wisdom of the Ghost King; otherwise, who knows how long it would have taken Archeron to reach this level?

After the Ghost King obtained the divine stone left behind by the Lord of Death, using his wisdom and strength, he was able to organize the world and plan the future of the realm. Everyone followed suit and joined the Ghost King.

After all, there was not much to do, and it was quite boring. Providing them with purpose was sufficient to garner the faith of all, making effecting change effortless.

From the once sparse land, many cities and towns appeared, making it no different from the mortal world in the ways it operated. One could find clothing stores, bars, and temples scattered in each city.

It was the first time in many years that many had the chance to live again.

In each city, one could find four palaces: the Lord Palace, the Mission Palace, the Ghost Catcher Palace, and the Prison Palace.

The capital city was the only place that had a King Palace, where the divine mountain and the Ghost King resided.

The Lord Palaces were directly under the command of the King Palace, with the Ghost Lords being in charge of the operation of their cities and the goings on within.

The Ghost Catcher Palace was tasked with capturing ghosts in the mortal world. With the permission of the Ghost King, they had the ability to travel between the two worlds.

The Prison Palace was where all the ghosts who were captured were held to be interrogated and to confess everything they had done when they were alive.

The Mission Palace was the core of the palaces, apart from the King's Palace. That was where ghosts could go to obtain missions; whether that was building roads or catching ghosts, they could be found here.

Every time they saw this scene, they could not help but marvel at the brilliance of their King. Even if someone else had obtained the divine stone, they were not sure they could create all this within such a short time.

Walking through the city square, they spotted many stores on the way, each selling unique products in Archeron. Many ghosts could be seen using ghost paper and coins to purchase wares.

If not for the moonlight shining down, one might have confused this place for the mortal world because of how similar they were. Apart from being ghosts and humans, the two were not so different.

Life and death were simple mirrors, reflecting each other.

It did not take long to appear in front of a tall white palace that seemed to overshadow the buildings around it.

Outside the doors, two Ghost Soldiers could be seen standing guard, ensuring that everyone followed the rules.

The line to the Mission Palace stretches outside the building, making them lament the wait.

"If we had completed this mission, we would have become level two Ghost Catchers."

The leader was also disappointed. They have done many missions together over the last year and have reached the last step for a promotion. It was a bit unfortunate that the guy was so slippery. However, instead of saying that, he said, "It is not a big deal; we will have many opportunities in the future. It might not have been a bad thing; after all, we have been working so much that we can use this time to relax. Didn't you just get married, Nico?"

Nico replied with a smile on his round face, "I did, but without the money from the mission, it is going to be hard to do anything fun."

The other guy wrapped his arms around his friend and teased, "Jonas, do not listen to him. You know this guy is a money grabber; he probably has many things put away in the bank or something."

Embarrassed, Nico tried to push his friend away, but to no avail, "I have to save and be wise about how I spend. I am trying to surprise her by moving to the city. It would be easier to get there that way. Don't think I didn't see how you were looking at that girl, Dahn. If it continues, it won't be long before you turn into me."

Dahn laughed but did not say anything.

As they were talking, the line moved, and it was not long before they reached the receptionist. Taking one of the parchments in front of him, Jonas wrote down what happened on the mission and gave it to the receptionist, who took the paper and placed it on a stack at her side.

The three of them turned to leave but were stopped by the receptionist.

"There are some people who are waiting for you; please follow me." The receptionist said that and told them to follow behind her.

She opened a side door and let them through. They walk for a few minutes before arriving in front of a large door with the insignia of the Mission Palace, a crawling tortoise.

On their way there, the three were confused. Who could be waiting for them, especially in the Mission Palace? They did not have the connection to warrant such a favor. Suppressing their doubts, they pushed open the door and entered, only to hear the door close behind them.

Taking a second to examine the room, they noticed a long table in the center, surrounded by chairs. On the walls, beautiful paintings of landscapes were hanging.

Sitting at the table, they saw four figures. These figures caused their breath to be stifled with shock and worry.

At the head of the table sat a middle-aged man wearing a golden robe with a crown on his head. His eyes were deep and seemed to gleam with tangible wisdom.

To his right, there was a beautiful woman with long black hair and limped eyes, wearing a red dress that seemed to wrap around her body too closely, exposing her nose bleeding curves. She had a small black dot resting at the corner of her left eye, which only further enhanced her beauty. A white necklace with a blue gemstone was hugging her neck.

In front of the beauty in red, a stack of papers was placed in an orderly manner.

Looking at the insignia of a crawling tortoise on her red dress, they immediately knew this was the Mission Lord!

The dressing requirements for any of the palaces were quite strict, with the Mission Palace choosing to wear white.

On the left of the man sitting at the head of the table, two other figures sat. One was an old man with droopy skin wearing a blue robe with the insignia of a tongue being cut by a sword. His fingers were covered in rings of many different colors.

The last figure was a young man with a powerful-looking body. His eyes were piercing, and his face was grim. He was wearing a black robe with chains at his waist and a scythe on his back. Even without looking at the insignia, they knew this was their boss, the Ghost-Catching Lord!

If everyone here is a palace lord, then the man in blue was perhaps the Prison Lord, the most feared of the three.

If that were the case, only one person could sit at the head of the table when these figures appear together: the Ghost King, Xeros!

Things seemed to take a lot of time, as if everything were moving in slow motion, but in reality, only a few seconds passed.

Dropping to their knees without hesitation, the three of them spoke their greetings: "Greetings, Your Majesty. Greetings, My Lords and Lady." The back of the hands and neck could not help but feel chilly. They were uncertain why these esteemed figures would summon some lowly Ghost Catchers, but they dared not question them.

These figures held the entirety of Archeron in their hands. If they offend them, it would be hard to get out alive.

The man at the head of the table, Ghost King Xeros, nodded. "There is no need for formalities; come here and have a seat."

"Yes, Your Majesty." While nervous, the three sat at the other end of the table, keeping a couple of meters between them. It was already an honor to sit at the same table; they did not dare to sit too close.

The worry and confusion they hid earlier seemed eager to come out. They could not help but reflect on their past actions, trying to figure out if they did anything that would warrant this sudden scene. Their conscience was clear; they had not broken any laws, so their fear lessened somewhat once they were aware of this. However, they were still nervous.

"There is no need to be nervous; we did not call you here to punish you." The words of the Ghost King reached their ears and slightly calmed their nerves.

"Iris."

Iris, the Mission Lord, bowed her head slightly and said, "Thank you, My Lord. Before we continue, I would like to apologize for the method we used to contact you. This was very important, and delays were not on the agenda. Now, I believe your names are Jonas, Nico, and Dahn, correct?"

Jonas nodded but immediately realized that might be rude and spoke, "Yes, My Lady."

Iris nodded and continued, "Our records showed that you three are level one Ghost Catchers; is that correct?"

The confusion between Jonas and the rest was becoming clear, but they still answered, "That is correct, My Lady. We have not been able to rank up as we have not been able to catch the required amount of ghosts."

Dahn, the usual happy-go-lucky guy, spoke in a cautious tone, "My Lady, we have also not been able to harness our ghost power to the required level. But we believe it will not be too long before we can."

"Mmm." Iris frowned as she looked at the paper and glanced at them. "Our records show the same. However, how despite this level of ghost power, are you able to capture so many powerful ghosts? In our records, it shows that you three have captured more than 50 ghosts within the last year. Even those of higher rank than you cannot do this, so how can you?"

"..."

The three did not know how to respond. The questions did not make sense to them. What powerful ghost? If they were powerful, how could they catch them? They want to know too!

Feeling the silence, Xeros said, "We are not doubting you; we are simply confused. As you know, Archeron is able to absorb weak ghosts, but if they exceed a certain limit, we must capture them and bring them back. Which is the reason for the Ghost Catchers."

The three were still confused, but Nico answered, "Your Majesty, we have not done anything different from what we learned in our training. We indeed came across ghosts, but we were not aware they were that powerful. As soon as we appear in the mortal world, we simply use our ghost chains to bind them or our scythe to the injured before capturing them. We have not faced any situation that would make us think they were powerful."

The Ghost Catcher Lord, Tobias looked at Xeros and spoke, his voice booming, "My Lord, I have examined the ghost they brought, and it is just as they said. Not only that, these three passed the course to become Ghost Catchers with nearly perfect scores; I do not think they would have placed themselves in a situation that they cannot handle. Dahn is quite cautious; if he felt it was a powerful ghost, he would have reported it."

Xeros nodded slightly, still deep in thought. On the three's last mission, he had Tobias observe the three but they did everything according to the standards; there was nothing odd about them. However, that did not explain how they could capture these powerful ghosts.

Even with a rough estimate, these ghosts could rival some Ghost Lords, which was not something they could achieve, even if there were a hundred of them.

Even though the ghosts in the mortal realm couldn't access ghost power without absorbing the power inside Archeron, this bridge couldn't be closed with tiny Ghost Catchers with barely any control over their ghost powers.

In the development stage of Archeron, a genius appeared who was able to discover the mystery of the moonlight energy within the realm. Absorbing it would grant access to a peculiar power with mysterious effects known as ghost power.

With the new source of power, ranks were created to differentiate the different levels of purity of energy a ghost possesses. Regular Ghost, Ghost Soldier, Ghost Catcher, Ghost Lord, Palace Lords, and Ghost King.

Each of these ranks has far more power than the last.

Currently, if Xeros had to estimate his current power, he would say he might have half the power that the Lord of Death showed that day. It is a rough estimate, but he believed it was close enough.

For a Ghost Lord-level ghost to be captured by Ghost Catchers, obviously many eyebrows would be raised, which is why it reached his desk in his palace. Even now, he could not sense anything above a Ghost Catcher from these three, making him believe their words. Well, he believed Tobias's words, but there was no need to point that out.

"My Lord, if I may speak," the tactirin Prison Lord, Theo, said.

"Go ahead."

"Thank you, My Lord. The credibility of their words should be high. After speaking to those ghosts, they mention they were attacked by someone, and when they woke up, they were in prison. So perhaps someone attacked them before the Ghost Catchers arrived? I think that would explain everything."

Xeros frowned and found that if it were as Theo said, everything would make perfect sense, but… "So you are saying someone in the mortal world is helping us capture ghosts? What do they hope to gain by doing so? Even if there was some kind of gain, we still do not know who it was. It is unknown if they are friends or foes. Just because they have not attacked us does not mean this will always be the case. We must find out who it is."

"Yes, My Lord." Everyone bowed their heads; even the trio did.

Iris wrote down some things on a piece of paper as Xeros was speaking, looking like a dutiful secretary.

With an apologetic expression, Xeros said to the three, "Thank you for coming and answering our questions. I heard your report to the receptionist; do not worry; Iris is currently working on it."

"It was no problem, Your Majesty; we are happy to help." The three of them got up and bowed, knowing that was their cue to leave.

Watching the door close behind the three, Xeros looked at the officials of his court, his aura towering over them. Unlike before, with his calm and easy-going facade, he became like a hungry beast, waiting to devour his prey whole.

"Tobias, reward those three. From the reports, it is clear they are hard working. Also, make sure they do not spread anything we discussed today."

Tobias got up and knelt down as his name was called.

"It shall be done."

Standing up from his seat, Xeros's figure broke apart and disappeared from the room, his voice lingering like a whisper: "Iris, I need you to select a capable person and create a new palace. This will be responsible for gathering information. This will no longer be your responsibility. Send me a report with any ideas you may have at the next meeting."

The other two palace lords knelt down in the direction of the King's Palace. "Yes, my Lord. Farewell."

CHAPTER 14

AUGUST

(Unknown Location)
(Year 257 of the Tribunal Calendar, Month of the Cancer)

Inside a room lit by candlelight, a tall man wearing a white cloak with elbow-length gloves could be seen walking down a line of cages with a notepad in his hand.

Shriek!

Looking at the mice who were twitching uncontrollably, August, with an indifferent look in his eyes, wrote 'failure' in the notepad.

He did not stop his stride and kept observing all the animals in the cages with slight expectations in his deep eyes.

It did not take long before he arrived in front of a cage with a pig inside, which seemed to have not suffered much under the experiment.

Looking at the information on the notepad, August looked at the pig, a feeling of happiness washing over him. He had succeeded! Although it was one out of a hundred, it proved that his hypothesis was correct.

August had been conducting research for many years, hoping to create an undying race that would continually grow without succumbing to death.

Just this thought was obscured; it was something he found he could not succeed in, even after decades. The more he thought of it, the more obsessed he became with figuring it out.

Writing something on the notepad, he walked back over to his desk and sat down. He felt extremely exhausted; it had been so long since he actually sat down.

Knowledge has been his driving force. There was so much to learn but so little time to do it. Even though he could live longer than other people thanks to his experiment, eventually he too would die, meaning his experiments would come to a halt.

Opening his eyes, August noticed a golden drop of blood within a glass bottle on his desk, and his eyes shone.

His longtime friend, Maria, had sent a drop of blood to him to examine and determine if it was possible to fuse with. He was somewhat baffled by this request, especially when it came from Maria, who has always had a skeptical view of this side of the world.

Out of everything he had experimented on so far, this was by far the most precious one. No matter how he looked at it, he couldn't understand how such a tiny drop of blood had so much vitality.

He had fused the blood with animals, but none of them could withstand the vitality in the blood, which eventually exploded. Even after exploding, the animals' blood recondenses into a drop. It cannot be fused with, nor could it be destroyed; it was truly fascinating in how it came to be.

Thoughts of asking Maria where it came from crossed his mind, but August decided not to inquire about it. While they were friends, they were not close enough to dig into each other's business deeper than necessary.

One thing was certain, though: this blood did not belong to a human. No human could possess such powerful blood. Though it was possible that not only the blood was like this, the muscles, organs, and bones probably possessed the ability to withstand it.

Through some research and cross-reference, August concluded that a human could indeed fuse with this blood, but they would definitely die in the end. Though not the answer he wanted to give his friend, he was never one to lie.

As he sat there in his own world, the sounds of gears began to move as the contraption to go up and down from his underground lair moved.

August was not concerned about this, as only one of his experimental subjects had access to it. There was no possibility of betrayal, so he had even less reason to be worried.

As someone who delved into the darkness, he was not fondly looked upon by most people. The temples were even more repulsed by him and often sent people out to kill him, but he was always one step ahead.

These people who called him a devil were more sinister than they appeared. They sent people to kill him, but they only wanted to obtain the results of his research.

Everyone wanted to live forever, and with August as living proof of his research, it would be odd if they were not tempted.

However, the times have changed. Unlike in his younger days, he was not capable of running around, making the need for an underground base even more important.

The gears stopped turning, and two doors opened, allowing a small man with a slightly deformed face to walk in. He was wearing a white uniform and slightly limped to the side when he walked.

Arriving before August's desk, the man bowed. "Master, I have followed your orders and discovered some things have happened since your seclusion."

August looked up with confusion and expectations written all over his face. If he calculated correctly, he had only been here for around 13 years, give or take, so things were bound to change. However, his experimental subject would not report minor things going on. Even if a powerful person were to be killed, he would not have reported it. Not because it was not shocking news, but because it brought no benefit to know about it.

He was expectant because of the many changes in the mouth of his experimental subject. As time went on and his lifespan continued to shrink, it was getting harder and harder to acquire knowledge and conduct research. He did not have much time left, maybe a year or two.

While his body appeared to be in his youth, August was more than a hundred years old. The experiment had pushed his lifespan to this stage, but it came with side effects. His flesh was starting to decay at an alarming rate, making it harder and harder to move.

Even his mind was getting cloudy at times. There were signs that death was closing in on him.

Unlike others, August, who has been in close proximity to death for most of his life, did not fear it. People fear death because they do not know what exists after. Would they cease to be? Would everything they made fade? Would anyone remember them?

These thoughts to him were quite vain and pointless. The living should be prepared for death the moment they are born. Just like how humans die, one day this world will also experience the same thing.

August's thoughts on death were quite different. In his view, even if he was close to death, it did not matter much. He had only had one goal throughout his life: creating the undying race, and while he had only been taking small steps so far, it had fulfilled his wish. The only pity he had was that this dream might never be achieved.

From the beginning to the end, undying was a flawed concept that did not exist. What makes a race undying? Living forever and achieving the pinnacle of physical prowess? No, Undying didn't mean any of those.

Undying is meant to escape from life and death and live in the middle.

"Go on."

"Yes, Master. Although many people are not aware, I was able to gather these bits and pieces of information. The first piece, I think, will interest you. Recently, many strange things have been happening in Pylos City State, one of which is the introduction of a new occupation called "Mages". While I was not able to gather much about them, I have learned they can use mystical powers and have a longer lifespan than others. I think if you can become a Mage, you could perhaps solve your situation."

August was somewhat surprised by this information. Mystical powers and a long lifespan? This was fascinating to him, but he couldn't help but wonder how he had never discovered this secret throughout his life.

While he did not claim to know everything, he knew a lot. Mystical powers were not something this world had, well, apart from the gods and monsters. For humans to use such powers and not be demigods was quite interesting.

If he could become a Mage, August thought he would enjoy it, especially since they granted him a longer lifespan. While he did not fear death, if he could live longer and explore more wonders, he wanted to give it a shot.

Only a fool would want to die when there was an opportunity to live.

"Have you located these Mages? Or have you found a way to become one?"

The deformed man shook his head and said, "I am sorry, Master; these Mages are quite hard to track down. Even after many days of searching, I was not able to find one and learn of the methods for you."

August felt it was a pity, but he was not too worried about it. Since the Mages already appeared once, it was only a matter of time before it would happen again. Plus, with his intelligence, as long as he had a clue to becoming a Mage, he could slowly find a way for himself.

Looking at his subordinate, August was quite thankful he conducted that experiment; otherwise, it is very likely he would have missed this precious information.

Resurrecting the corpse of a young child and embedding him with many experimental liquids to bring him back to life was a fluke, but the outcome was a loyal subordinate who placed his needs above anything else.

It was a pity this was a failure; even though he brought the body back to life, it was not the same child that died. August was not sure why that was the case, but perhaps it had to do with what makes a person a person. Unfortunately, even after researching and experiencing many things, he was not able to understand this illusionary field.

"What else?"

"Master, I heard rumors that Argos and Cornith might be going to war soon. Although I do not know the reason, it seems the land might be filled with chaos soon."

War on the horizon? He was no stranger to war, having lived through many conflicts. In fact, the more wars there were, the faster and more results he got during his research. The bodies of the dead are easier to work with than the living. No need to be careful; just do it until you cannot anymore.

However, while he does not mind war, August smells a conspiracy brewing. Argos, to his knowledge, although strange in the way it operated, was a very powerful city-state with a powerful force.

If he had to rank the strongest city-states, it would be Athens, Sparta, Corinth, Thebes, and Argos.

Many people might have laughed at the thought that Athens was a place above Sparta, but Athens was very powerful. They had knowledge and military powers that exceeded those of Sparta, which only focused on military might.

He could not see why such a powerful city-state would attack a city-state so far away. Not only would this draw the attention of Athens and Sparta, who were close by, but things might spiral out of control and become something they could not control.

There were many city-states surrounded by these giants, so who was to say they would not pick a side, turning the tide of the war?

Originally, he was going to steal some resources while the chaos spread, but the more he thought about it, the more worried and scared he became.

This war might not have been instigated by either Argos or Corinth; there might be some force behind the scenes.

CHAPTER 15

SEALED REALM

(Year 257 of the Tribunal Calendar, Month of the Cancer)

Oblivious that his blood was in August's laboratory, Archeus closed in on the area that Archeron brushed when it was in the process of expanding.

Originally, he planned on going to the location after spreading the way of magic, but one thing after another happened. Athena's descent did not improve the situation either.

Using Archeron's influence on Arctara as a guide, Archeus descended to the location by teleporting from Tiamat.

Although his divine ability in space was powerful, Archues could not teleport to somewhere he had never been before. For example, if he was in area A and wanted to go to area B, he had to see the area first, as he needed the coordinates.

Once he had the coordinates, it did not matter how much time went by; he would be able to descend to the area, as he would subconsciously remember the coordinates.

Although this seemed to be a flaw in his power, it was the only one, so in the end, it all depended on the way one looked at things. If he were in a dangerous situation and needed to teleport away, just the fact that he would only be teleported to places he had been would be an advantage.

If, when he teleports, he arrives at a random place, Archeus would not dare use Teleportation as he has. He was not the only powerful being in this world; there were many who surpassed him. While they have not shown their true faces yet, it didn't take a genius to see they were not on good terms.

With his eyes glowing a deeper shade of gold, Archeus looked at the empty space in front of him with a frown.

To others, the space in front of Archeus was no different than any other place. However, to him, who was a master of space, the scene was different.

In his eyes, Archeus saw a deep hole that was created from space. The hole was not large, maybe a meter or so in size but this hole was gaping, leading to some unknown location.

What made him frown was not the space, but the power surrounding it. The power was faint blue; one could vaguely hear the sound of waves from it. The dwindling power explained why Archeron could locate this unknown area in space.

In Archeus mind, this power was similar to his divine power, but it was different as he could hear something else within the waves: faith.

This power was clearly the work of a god of this world, which meant this energy was divine energy, whose reliance on faith was important.

There was only one God who ruled over water that came to mind, but Archeus wind went back to the conversation with Athena, and his frown deepened. Perhaps he was only being told one part of a story, while he was giving them far more than they were letting on.

It didn't matter; he did not lose anything; if anything, he was bound to gain something.

Waving his hand at the space, the blue divine energy vanished, and the space became stable, creating a passage into its depths.

Flying through the passage, with layers and layers of space flickering around his body as protection, Archeus indifferently entered the passage.

While his action could be considered impulsive, Archeus felt he did not have a choice. If he remained in Tiamat and allowed an unknown passage in his area of influence, who knew when it would come back to bite him in the ass?

He would never underestimate the gods, that was for certain. This was clearly their work; what purpose it served was unknown.

He was not worried about his safety because he had already achieved trifold immortality. Although he cannot face a major god like Athena head-on, he surpasses the level of a demigod. It doesn't matter if it was Zeus or Gaia; they were not capable of bypassing the immortality granted by Eternal Vigor.

Archeus was starting to feel like Sun Wukong. The monkey king also used his immortality as the basis for his actions, but Archeus felt he was a bit smarter. At the very least, he strategizes meticulously.

While his immortality did give him confidence, his powers were what he relied on the most. In fact, unlike Maria, who got her powers from the Innate Divine System, the source of his is still a mystery. The most likely answer would be Earth, but since he cannot return there, he cannot be certain.

Walking through the passage, Archeus could feel the space around him tremble, seemingly under a lot of pressure. It did not seem to be on the verge of collapse, which proves his theory. A god was responsible for this passage.

But if Archeus could pass through while having merely half the strength of a true god, then it means the being who created this passage did not create it for himself. After all, the passage was already shaking under his pressure; how much more would it be under a god from Olympus?

Not only that, it didn't make sense for any god to reside inside it since they couldn't exist without faith, so it limited many of the options.

Exiting the passage, Archeus found himself in the skies of a world whose skies were pitch black with no stars. The ground was barren with cracks from a severe drought and harsh weather.

Although the world was dark, in his eyes, there was no difference between night and day. After all, he was a god. If such a thing could bother him, he would not have claimed such a title.

"I cannot sense the Weave, Tiamat, or Archeron. How far did this passage send me?" Archeus was surprised. He originally believed the passage would take him to another part of the Arctara, but that does not seem to be the case.

Even if he were in another location of Arctara, he would still be able to sense and locate his realms. The Weave has spread a larger distance than Tiamat and Archeron since it relied on absorbing energy from outside the world to continuously grow.

Even if he was in a different world, Archeus did not have many worries. If anything, he could simply rewind time and go back to before he entered the world.

However, time control was something he was not exactly good at. To go back a second, he must expend a lot of divine power. Maybe when he becomes stronger, he can use it as he likes, but for now, it is an iffy situation.

This gave him a wake-up call. Even if he was prepared, things can go beyond what he expected. Imagine if it was Maria that came to this world and the passage closed; it was obvious she would be trapped here until the Weave extended to this location. That could take a couple of years or even a billion.

Closing his eyes and using the Over Element in conjunction with his space divine ability, Archeus realized this world was on the verge of death. The air was empty, with barely any oxygen. The land had no water or food, so it was incredible that it could support anything.

Even though this world was in a dire state, it was still in far better shape than Earth. Compared to Earth, which was like hell, it might as well have been heaven.

Sigh.

Archeus, with a rough estimate, saw that there were probably around a hundred or so creatures still alive.

The degree of life force varied, but it appeared that this world did not affect them in the same way as others.

To survive for this long was a testament to their strength and adaptability.

Unfortunately, neither Tiamat nor Archeron were present; otherwise, it would have been simple to identify these creatures.

Unleashing his full power, Archeus used it to scan the entire world and was once again surprised. The world was probably the same size as the Northern Highlands, with many mountains and dried-up rivers and oceans.

At each corner of the world, there was a pillar that stretched into the skies. It just happened that the location he descended to was the exact center between these pillars.

Although he could not see the pillars, he could sense them, the same as he did with the creatures of this world. There was an infinite amount of power within the pillars, which shocked Archeus.

The so-called power was faith! The amount of faith reached astonishing levels! If he were to absorb this faith, he could easily rival Chief Gods like Zeus. He was very tempted to try, but he restrained himself. It was not worth it. Unlike Athena and the rest, he was not a faith god. While he could absorb it, it did not really mean much to him.

Even without faith, his power was slowly increasing. He had a faint premonition that this gradual increase would not stop anytime soon.

The faint sound of waves came from the pillars, along with soft whispers of prayers.

Although he didn't know the full picture, it was clear that someone had sealed this world with the intention of preventing this faith from escaping. However, what Archeus could not understand was: how was it possible? Even in Tiamat, faith could reach him, so how did they do it?

He did not sense the presence of a god, so the god was not here. So why?

As Archeus was lost in thought, the creatures that were barely hanging on rushed towards the towering aura in the distance. If it were before the world became like this, maybe they would not dare approach, but right now, they do not have a choice. If they stayed away, they would die, but if they approached, there was a faint possibility of surviving.

Archeus looked in the distance, seeing some faint dots flying in the air towards him and, on the ground, dust clouds kicking up as a group of creatures entered his sight.

In the skies, there were two black dragons, one small and one large, and a dozen or so beautiful women with red hair and red eyes flying with their red wings. If one looked at these women quickly, the image of a battlefield and massacre would subconsciously appear.

On the ground, there were many tiny-looking humans wearing armor and riding giant wolves.

Archeus couldn't believe the scene. Why did this world look more like a fantasy world than Arctara?

Black Dragons are powerful beasts on the same level as demigods. The longer they live, the stronger they will become. Although they were not as strong as the Five Colored Dragons or the Supreme Dragons, alongside Thunder Dragons, Time Dragons, and Space Dragons, they were powerful.

Furies are maidens who are children of Primordial Gods, meaning they were goddesses just far weaker than even demigods. They serve Ares on the battlefield, causing mayhem and death wherever they go.

Dwarves are the best metalsmiths in a fantasy world, even rivaling gods. No matter what story one looked at, finding a dwarf was like finding a divine weapon in hand.

What else could the large wolves be if not Werewolves? They took the form of large wolves instead of the typical partial wolf transformation.

It is unknown if they were cursed by Zeus or not, but it's interesting either way.

Seeing the group congregating beneath him, Archeus landed on the ground, looking at them. Maybe because they were used to the darkness, it seemed they could easily see him.

The largest black dragon, who seemed to be the leader of the group, spoke, its voice guttural and deep. The darkness seemed to tremble faintly as it spoke but did not disappear, as even the Black Dragon could do nothing about it.

Lowering his large head, the dragon spoke, "My Lord, I am Gyrsyra, the Black Lord. I can see you are not a god of Olympus. If you can take us out of here, we are willing to serve you. With my strength, as long as it is not a god, I can be of use. My wife is a bit weaker, but she is also powerful. Everyone here is powerful in their own right; there is no disadvantage."

Archeus did not respond immediately, but the image he had in his mind of dragons being arrogant shattered in his mind. He could understand why they were like this, but why couldn't they do it differently?

As for their offer, Archeus did not plan to refuse. Before they suggested it, he was planning to send them to Arctara. Only when the world changes can he enjoy the benefits.

"I hear your words, but tell me, why were you guys sealed? If I release you, I will become an enemy of Olympus." While he did not know the reason why they were sealed, Archeus wanted to know. Even though he talked about the threat of Omlypus, he was not worried. It was still unclear how they would react to what he told Athena. Even if they'd become his enemies, it would not be because of this realm.

Ever since he understood the purpose of the Innate Divine System, he was not as excited when he saw or thought about fantasy creatures.

Gyrsyra's eyes seemed to be looking back in the past, reminiscing, "The main reason we were sealed was because of the dangers we brought to the human race. Around 5,000 years ago, when the gods and monsters roamed the world, a god created the human race. From there, the gods forwent the method of divinity they were born with in order to absorb faith, which quickly increased their divine energy. However, the monsters were in the way of their faith, so they were captured and sealed us in many small worlds."

So the main cause was faith again? But what was the difference between the faith provided by humans and that of monsters? There didn't seem to be a difference; hence, there was no reason to seal the monsters, as that would be counterproductive.

Although he already had an idea of who sealed them, Archeus asked, "So you have been sealed 5,000 years ago; do you know which god did it?"

Gyrsyra shook his giant reptile head. "No. All I know is that God must have been extremely powerful. Although we are all that remain of the monsters that were sealed in this world, there were many monsters who were stronger than me who died."

Nodding, Archeus already knew he would not get an answer but was still a little disappointed.

"Don't worry, I'll send you to Arctara. I do not need you to be loyal to me; just live as you please."

Originally, he was planning on fusing this world into Arctara, but it was not feasible because of the pillars filled with faith. There was obviously a force behind the scenes of this world that was able to plot against even the major gods.

While he couldn't be truly killed, Archeus knew there were many ways for him to suffer. And for the person who plotted against a main god and succeeded, they could do the same to him.

He refrained from disclosing his name out of fear. If they knew his name and plotted against him, he would not know how to react.

When they arrive in Arctara, the gods will obviously be aware that they have been released. And while there would be suspicions cast on him, that was all. Archeus had learned to mask his presence so that not even the gods could locate him, so he was not worried.

Not hesitating anymore, Archeus pointed in front of him, and a rift in space appeared, leading to Arctara.

"You can enter, and you will escape this cage."

Everyone bowed their heads with gratitude. "Thank you, my Lord; we will never forget this grace."

Taking a step, Archeus appeared before the divine pillar and examined it.

He didn't plan to take the pillar, but he figured since the gods might become his enemies he might learn a thing or two from it.

Observing the pillar for a couple of minutes, Archeus frowned as he didn't discover anything. Apart from the immense faith inside of it, the pillar did not seem any different from a regular piece of wood.

While it was a pity to leave without learning anything, Archeus was not upset. He already gained more than he expected; hoping for more is being greedy.

Taking a step, he disappeared from the small world and appeared back in Arctara before ascending to Tiamat.

The moment Archeus disappeared, the white pillar flickered, causing runes to appear. The runes flashed, with fine cracks spreading before disappearing as soon as they appeared.

A whisper escaped the piller, spreading across the abandoned land: "Poseidon… please… respond.."

CHAPTER 16

TENSIONS IN ALL DIRECTIONS

(Year 257 of the Tribunal Calendar, Month of the Cancer)

In a realm covered in golden light and clouds, a huge mountain could be seen hanging within the heavens.

Unlike the usual calmness that was present on this mountain, today it was filled with noise and conversation reaching every corner of the realm.

At the peak of the mountain, there was a white temple with twelve thrones. Many of the thrones were empty, with only four of them currently occupied.

On a dark throne, a middle-aged man is draped in a dark cloak that seems to have been created from darkness. On his head was a white bone helmet, which made him look even more ominous and secretive. His head was filled with long black hair, and his eyes were gentle and calm, without ripples.

At the side of his throne, leaning against it, was a two-prong spear.

On another throne was a beautiful woman wearing a golden battle skirt and shirt. She had a head filled with golden locks and deep golden eyes that shone with wisdom. Her face was calm, almost emotionless, as she stared at her companions. At her waist is a sword, and at her feet is the shield of a Medusa.

Directly across from her was a man with red hair and fiery eyes. His towering body screams brute force and power. His entire chest was exposed, showing off his rock-hard muscles. His hands were covered by armor, and his head was hidden underneath a helmet with red flames. His lower body was covered in armored pants. On his feet were spiked shoes.

At the base of his throne, there were two bastard swords that were covered in an ominous and dark hue. If one listened closely, they could faintly hear the screams of those who had fallen at their edges.

On the last throne, there was a man wearing white robes whose presence seemed to command the light around him. His long, shiny golden hair was flowing without wind. His golden eyes seem to be two suns, striking pain in the eyes of those who dare to look at him.

Unlike the rest, he did not have a weapon at the base of his throne, only a golden carriage with two lions inscribed on all sides.

The middle-aged man, covered in darkness, asked in a gentle tone, "Athena, what do you think of this fellow?

You spoke so highly of him and wanted us to work with him, but not even a month later, he released monsters back into Arctara. Does he not know how much effort was taken to seal them?"

Athena did not know what to say to this. Her conversation with Archeus was nice and straightforward. She got the answers she wanted, and that was good enough to satisfy the others, but who would have thought he would release monsters into Arctara?

In the past, when the gods led by Zeus took control of the world from the Titans, there were monsters who existed, not created by any beings. They simply existed, with many rivaling the strongest of the gods.

Although the creatures' release posed no threat to them, the same could not be said about the mortals. Even the Tribunal could not stand against them, especially the two black dragons.

The towering man with red hair and red eyes angrily looked at his sister. "Why must we work with this mortal? We have seen his power reach the heights of some lesser gods in such a short amount of time, and yet we do nothing! Could you not see he is a threat to us?"

Athena coldly responded, "Ares, you are not fooling anyone! You simply want to fight him."

"So what?! I am the God of War! I can clearly see that he will become our enemy; should it not make sense to eliminate him first?!"

The middle-aged man spoke, "I must agree with Ares. Even though he said he would not become our enemy and wanted to work with us, how can we be sure? We do not have control over him, but he has control over us. As long as he changes his mind and removes our faith in Arctara, we will become meat on a chopping block."

All eyes fell on Athena, causing her to feel pressured. Everything they said was true, but from interacting with Archues in person, she saw he was genuine. However, Archeus was once a human, so he might change his mind if he felt the gods would become a threat to him.

The image of him showing interest in her made Athena confident that he would not harm her. His goal was simple, and unless there was an extreme cause, there was no reason for the scene Hades mentioned to happen.

Athena was aware she was basing much of her thoughts on 'ifs'. In divine strategies, there were no ifs. However, while they watched Archeus grow, they truly didn't know much about him. If they attacked him now, it would not stop or change the fact that they were slowly losing faith.

"Whether he becomes our enemy or not, remember, while we hold the advantage now, in a hundred or even a thousand years, will we still exist? Currently, we have no choice but to join his plans."

Hades did not say anything and had a smile on his face. He already figured this would happen. Zeus had chosen to fall asleep, an action he hadn't taken since the gods' faith began to wane, until now. It was obvious that Zeus was hopeful that something would change this issue.

Apollo looked at the scene but did not say anything. Unlike the others, he was not lacking in faith at all. His domain was very vast, meaning he had a vast ocean of followers to worship him.

However, his sister and mother, Artemis and Leto, fell asleep many years ago, making him quite worried. They did not possess good domains that didn't overlap with popular gods and goddesses, making them weak even when compared to some of the lesser gods.

Apollo saw hope in the mortal after hearing Athena's account. If his mother and sister could join this mortal, it was very likely they would regain their faith and wake up.

Since he had already made his decision, there was not much left for him to say.

Ares was furious to see that everyone was on board, but he truly could not see a way to stop them. He truly wanted there to be a battle, as only then could he become stronger.

That was why he was instigating Argos and Corinth to fight. If the war could spread further, he would only be happier, but...

Looking at his sister, he became worried. If Athena saw benefits and even Hades was siding with her, it was unlikely for the information to be wrong. Unlike those who might benefit, it was unlikely for him.

Who would worship him apart from Sparta? No one! Not every mortal was eager for war, and no one would worship him. If the world this mortal spoke about became a reality, he might be one of the few gods who truly faded away from the world's stage.

The only thing he could do was speak to the mortal and find a way to survive, but if he did that, he would become the laughing stock of Olympus.

His father was a wise god and a good leader. His actions did not escape Ares' eyes. Everything Zeus did had deep meaning. And like the others, he was aware that Zeus was on the mortals' side, which made things clear to him.

Unless something disastrous happens, the fact that the gods would work with mortals would not change.

Just like the other gods, he had been observing the mortal and was excited when he created a new race. The more races there are, the more conflict! Even when he released those monsters, the probability of war only increased in Ares' eyes.

Thinking of this, resolve appeared in his eyes as he looked at Athena. "I would like to speak with this mortal; can you contact him for me?"

Athena looked at her brother with suspicion but did not refute it. "I can contact him, but I should warn you: don't go overboard."

Clenching his fist with anger and shame, Ares nodded.

Back at the Tribunal headquarters, a similar scene was taking place, with the Three Stars wearing serious expressions after sensing the presence of powerful beings in Eurasia.

However, unlike the gods, they were not sure who these beings were.

They could tell many of these beings rivaled them, which meant they were demigods, which was frightening to say the least! It took many years to create a demigod, but there were so many of them.

They did not have enough people to pose a threat!

What alarmed them even more was the silence of the gods. Usually, the gods would send down an oracle to them, but there was nothing but silence.

They were not certain if the gods had tacitly agreed to this or not.

Although, they could smell the scent of change on the horizon.

This could be an opportunity for them to become gods.

Tensions between Argoes and Corinth were becoming more serious as both cities were enlisted farmers within their military.

The surrounding factions were taking a wait-and-see approach but it was obvious they were thinking of grabbing some benefits once they saw it.

The surrounding city-states were muddying the waters by interacting with both factions, with many empty promises.

CHAPTER 17

DIVINE BATTLE

Back in Tiamat, Archeus reached into his pocket dimension and took out the piece of Athena's armor with confusion in his eyes.

Even in his pocket dimension, he could feel the fragment shaking like crazy, which caught his attention.

The fragment broke free from his hand and floated in the air, condensing a phantom image of Athena, who looked around the surroundings with curiosity in her eyes. She did not seem to notice the expression on Archeus' face.

Archeus did not imagine that Athena had this ability. What if she could use this fragment as a way to enter Tiamat when he isn't paying attention? This worried him greatly.

He thought he was becoming familiar with the power of the gods, but time and time again, he was proven to be naive. Even a small fragment could ignore his senses and be taken back by him. Who would have thought a god was hidden inside it?

"This is a nice world you have here. It reminds me of Arctara when it was still developing." Athena said with genuine emotion.

Archeus did not say anything. He was more nervous than he had ever been before. He did not seem to be as interested in Athena as he was in the beginning.

This was quite an interesting feeling. When he felt they were on equal footing, this feeling did not appear, but when things began to escape his control, that interest was replaced with fear.

Seemingly noticing this, Athena spoke, "I did not do this intentionally. My equipment has been with me for many years, so it possesses some of my divinity inside of it. Anyway, Ares, my brother wants to meet you, and since I did not want to call you on Arctara when things could be dangerous, I had no choice but to use this method."

Archeus sighed with relief but was confused about why Ares wanted to see him. He didn't seem to harm his interest, so there's no reason for them to meet.

"Why does he want to meet me?"

Athena shook her head. "I'm not sure about that, but it shouldn't be harmful to you. Most of the gods have agreed to work with you; I do not think Ares would be stupid to cross the line."

After thinking about it for a moment, Archeus decided to meet Ares. He figured he didn't have anything to lose if he didn't go, but since the gods were paying attention to him, he could not lose face.

"Okay, where does he want to meet?"

Athena once again shook her head. "I do not know. However, if I know my brother, he will probably want to fight you, so be prepared. If you go to Arctara and wait, I am sure he will find you."

The phantom of Athena began to dim and fade away.

Holding the fragment in his hand, Archeus placed layers and layers of space around it. He was not stupid enough to hold it when he did not know what else it could do.

A month passed since Athena intruded inside Tiamat, and Archeus was waiting above the open sea, fully covered in black armor and wielding a saber in his hand.

Although he has never used a saber before, considering his advantages, it only made sense to use a weapon that brings to light his true potential. Any other weapon would only be a hindrance.

"I am glad they finished it in time..."

He did not think he would make a request of the dwarves so soon, but he had them create his equipment for him earlier than he planned. The weapon and armor were quite good; even when he used his full power, he could not damage them in the slightest.

Archeus knew he would not be an opponent of Ares, but he did not plan to go down without a good fight. Plus, he was curious about this current strength. Since he became a god, he had never fought anyone, making him someone with power but no experience.

While flying in the air for a few minutes, the heavens opened, and from a bottomless maw, a tall man with red hair and red eyes descended. A bastard sword rested on his shoulder, and a blood-red aura around him persisted.

The stranger was partially covered in armor. His arms had armguards, up to his elbows. His torso was covered in chest plate and he wore leather pants with iron boots. Around his waist was a brown belt that secured his pants and joined the pants and the chest plate together, making it seem he was wearing a suit of armor.

"It is him…Ares.."

He had never met Ares before, but without a question, he knew this was him. Call it a gut feeling or whatever you like, but he was sure it was him.

With the arrival of Ares, the entire sky seemed to turn into a field of blood and gore as the God of War stood proudly in the skies!

The world trembled; echoes of battle arose, shaking the very heavens!

The wails of widows and the battle chants of men and women reverberated.

The echoes of loss and win and the rattling of weapons like a serenade played all around.

A slight hint of confusion flickered across Archeus' face, which was soon replaced by concern. Though he had no fear of death, he was aware he was not a match for Ares. As someone who stands at the same level as Athena, there is no way he can win.

Ever since Ares appeared, Archeus has been feeling a primal urge inside of him, roaring to battle against those stronger than him. He was certain this was what Ares was doing; after all, he was not a rash person.

There is no way I can overcome him! Should I retreat? There is no point to this anyway. NO! I cannot! If I turn back now, everything I have worked for will be for nothing!

"I will overcome him. To prove…"

His iron grip around his saber tightened, strangling the feeling of fear and weakness that threatened his will.

As someone who knows death intimately on Earth, while he tried to live as long as he could, he did not fear death. So while strange feelings appeared in his heart and mind, he did not act on them and instead remained relatively calm.

It was just in time! Before Archeus could even blink, Ares, who was quite a distance from him, appeared before him!

He was so close that Archeus could feel Ares' breath on his skin and could see the madness and bloodshed in his eyes.

Ares towered over him like Goliath, standing before David. It was definitely not how he imagined their first meeting.

"I am sure; Athena told you the reason I called you here." Archeus tried to look confident and unshaken, but looking into the eyes of what could be summed up as a sea of blood, even his mind trembled faintly, with cracks appearing on it.

"She shared your plan with us, a scheme that, in my view, lacks merit. So, tell me, mhm, your name is Archeus, correct?" Seeing Archeus nod, Ares continued, "Archeus, tell me, in the new world of yours, where would someone like me fit? A god who is not seen favourably by others. A divinity that is often favored by the bloodthirsty, the warmonger, the mad, and the tyrant. Answer me mortal!"

Archeus looked at the figure before him and gulped. He felt something strange, even confusing. Ares' voice was booming but calm. Carrying the might of a thousand swords! But hidden behind his words was a confusing tone. Uncertainty, and even fear? He was not sure he felt or interpreted it right.

It was odd, but somehow he could tell. The god came for answers, and he will get them, one way or another.

As for him? Archeus was confused as to why Ares wanted to fight. Archeus had been itching for a fight for a long time but never found anyone who would face him. Engaging Maria in combat, even in a sparring match, was beyond her capabilities due to the disparity in their skill levels. He could not fight Athena, as her stance was still unknown.

Hearing Ares' question, he was even more confused. Athena should have been aware of the world that will be born, so why was Ares here asking him? Whether it be gods of order or gods of chaos, Archues did not prefer any over the other. To him, the more there were, the better. Only with different gods could the world be more colorful.

"Ares, what manner of foo…"

As Archues was about to speak, the god of war welcomed him with a mighty punch in the chest, collapsing his chest plate, but the pressure even reached his chest and even his lungs!

If he were a mere mortal, this strike would have most likely ended him on the spot. He even questioned whether a punch of such potency could be survivable to a mere demigod.

"What manner...of foolish question is that?!" Alas, while not being a genuine god, he possessed the power to firmly sit amongst them. So, while the punch shattered his chest, it did not stop him from finishing his sentence.

Thrown quite a distance back, the hole on his chest gaping underneath the enchanted armor -- which dented itself back to shape -- started to close. Eternal Vigor was working overtime, trying to mend and fix anything out of place.

It was a mere blow from the God of War, an unarmed strike targeting his chest. The mere thought causes him to wonder if his armor could block the gods' blow. How could he even get close to a monster like that?!

"So strong...!"

He didn't have much more time to ponder the might of Ares because his instincts honed on Earth flared up, warning him of impending danger!

Was it a lucky guess or an instinct? Or do feelings come with practice?

It didn't really matter; the primitive part of his brain moved his hand and the blade, managing to deflect, or at least deflect, the screaming blood-red sword! A weapon that wailed with the anguish and mad laughter of the countless dead souls of the battlefield.

"Kch!" The bones in Archeus's hand cracked, even though he deflected the blow!

Just how powerful were the gods really?! A simple strike from Ares caused my hand to shatter and sent me flying. It was obvious he was not serious, with how lazy that strike was. It was not wrong to call him the Battle God of Olympus, he truly deserves this title!

"I can't give up…!"

Despite all the pain and agony, he forced his body to stop in the air and swung his blade out of sudden rage and defiance. His strike was blocked by the pommel of the enemy's weaponry, and in return for his rebellious act, Archues felt the mighty feet stomp on his chest, which once again collapsed his insides, splattering against the backside of his plate!

"Kuehh...!?"

His eyes bulged, almost falling out of their sockets! Heaving heavily, a large amount of golden blood spewed from Archeus mouth, falling into the tumbling waters below. But it was not the end, but the beginning of a quick combo that followed!

Before Archeus could understand what was going on, the momentum of Ares changed, and he suddenly landed over a hundred blows in a matter of seconds!

This was not a battle, but a beatdown between a war veteran and a glass cannon. It was easy to see who would have the upper hand.

It was not good! Archeus felt completely outmatched! Eternal Vigor was endless, but even it had a limit on how much it could repair his physical body at once! Like this, he would be chipped away little by little!

Each strike echoed across the skies! Each attacked a part of the sea, creating mighty storms, making the mortals wail in desperation, and praying for salvation on the lands close by!

Each blow tore a part of him; even his armor could barely repair the damage it received. Without it, he would be turned to a bloody pulp in mere moments.

"How does your blood taste, mortal? Warmed up enough? Ready to continue our spar?" Ares asked, planting his feet on the still regenerating Archeus after the seconds-long play -- which felt like an eternity.

At the bottom of the place, which was once a vast ocean, only the two of them are now present. The seas retreated far in the wake of Ares's mighty strikes! Leaving only the remnants of dead sea life!

Gasp!

Ares watched him wordlessly for seconds, waiting for his opponent to recover just enough so they might continue. His blood-churning eyes were cold, awaiting a firm answer.

"I…" Archeus opened his mouth, trying to form words with his slowly regenerating throat, yet the God of War preceded him, kicking him away.

"If this is all you can do, that plan is destined to fail. If that's the case, just give up. Or struggle alone; don't drag others into a failed endeavor."

That pitiful gaze, that dismissing frown! In some way, it infuriated Archeus more than anything! It hurt. He never thought the difference would be this big. Between a god of Tiamat and a god of Olympus, there is a vast distance. Ares was not even using all his power, probably less than what he has, and was stomping him to the ground!

What he lacked was obviously experience. He did not have these powers for a long time, but what about Ares? He has been a god since the time the world was formed. How much time did he have to learn and become the God of War he was today?

"You think…!?" With a swing of a sword, Archeus' jaw disappeared, searing pain worthy of a divine weapon coursed through his veins!

"I am not interested in your words. Discard your petty pride! Show me your worth by your actions, not by scheming like that sister of mine! If you can't shoulder the responsibility, I will destroy you myself! If your strength is lacking, I will throw you before my hounds to feast on your innards! If your drive is lacking, I will steal you in the deepest parts of Tartarus myself!"

At this moment, the God of War aura rose violently; his aura pushed away the clashing waves that were trying to fill the empty area in waters below, forcing them to leave once more in a violent clash of powers!

The land closest to the sea was placed under frightening pressure. Mortals pleaded and prayed, already considering an apocalypse was to come, because their foolish actions must have enraged the gods!

Archeus had chosen a location very far from any landmass in order to not harm the mortals, but the fact that Ares' power could still reach such a distance is shocking! He was not prepared for this! He never imagined Ares to be this powerful!

Regardless, he had to push forward! And when Ares kicked him away, he conjured his divine power, teleporting to Ares' side!

The saber, which was forged by the best dwarf smiths, sang its song as it cut through the air— even space itself! Pouring all his strength, hoping nothing but a mere shallow injury after what he had seen, Archeus made his move! His first true attack in this long combat!

"Hah! I see you have guts!"

Ares, however, was expecting such an assault! By merely leaning away, he grabbed Archeus's arm behind him, hitting his ribs by twisting his body to face him. Alas, that was supposed to happen, because in the last moment, Archeus called forth his shield, absorbing the impact.

Even though my shield?!

Alas, the result was unexpected! His eyes widened, feeling, as his arm turned to jelly, the resonance of the impact breaking the bones in his body!

The heavens and earth seem to shake under the weight of the impact. And Archeus could feel the blood in his body rushing towards his throat, filling his mouth!

The pain… but what's this rush?

Out of impulse, he spat the blood toward Ares' eyes, who welcomed it with a glint of a grin. Not dodging the spat! Not closing his eyes, but like a madman, forcing them to stay open, he made a step forth!

"Lesson one: never take your eyes off the opponent!"

Archeus' brows raised in fright and surprise, seeing the mighty fist coming in his direction! He had to teleport, or it would take his head off! He was sure of it!

"This is not good…"

By no means did his body react to his command, but the impact was still there in his destroyed face, even though it was out of reach!

Nothing more than the sheer force of the air and the touch of Ares' knuckles against his helmet were required to bring him to his knees and mold his headgear to his face.

But it was still odd—all that pain and agony each time a strike connects, yet why does he feel this excitement? Why does he feel this thrill? Is it possible because he is fighting Ares? The master of weapons and war? The father of martial power?

"Is your blood boiling yet, eh? How does it taste?"

He didn't get much more leeway because Ares swung his mighty blade just at the right distance to cut the bridge of his nose. Even teleporting backwards didn't save him completely from the swing!

"Lesson two: one's mind simply does not wander in battle."

Even though his injuries healed, he still felt some strange burning under his skin. That sword.. every time he got cut by it, a mere starch left a mark on his soul! His armor regenerated, but it barely dampened the strike! It was useful, but far from perfect!

He didn't even want to think about what would happen if Ares decided to use his weapon for real.

I have been defending myself ever since we met, I will never defeat him like this.

He concluded, and since the start of their standoff, he has searched for an opening while their battle has continued. But no matter how hard he tried, he saw no exploitable weakness or anything he could clamp on to at least get a good strike!

He tried every tactic his mind could come up with, but all were seen through and countered! Each mistake was grievously punished!

Is it possible he is seeing the future? Even such absurd theories resurfaced in his mind.

All manner of plans and strategies he can come up with were countered, preceded, and punished, leaving him little choice but to defend despite his intention to counterattack!

Was it possible that, despite his effort to take the initiative, he became the puppet that the puppet master played on?

While contemplating this, he banished his shield from his destroyed arm back to his pocket dimension, using Time and Space Control, calling back his saber to his repaired hand.

"Your mind wanders again! Foolish mortal! Have you learned nothing!?"

Ares puffed steamy impatience from his nostrils, seemingly not satisfied with his opponent's performance in the slightest.

For him, who even Zeus considered a dangerous opponent to face due to his martial prowess, a mere mortal turn god, was not giving his all? A blatant disrespect!

"Tceh…! Mediocre. The same thing again…"

Grabbing the blade coming from behind him barehanded, he twisted his body towards Archeus, who tried to strike his bare nape by teleporting behind him.

The divine blood dripped from Ares' crusty palm, yet he ignored the damage, twisting the blade from the boy's hand and following up with a right hook, which crushed Archeus' handsome visage into a pile of meat!

Amidst the crunch of bones and the gushing of his blood, Archeus strangely expected the attack, but he could simply not counter it! Somehow, the God of War outwitted him in every move and aspect! He moved faster, used simple yet effective moves, or put more power behind his strikes than he could ever calculate!

I feel he is barely putting any divine power in his attacks or defense. Then… why? How is it possible? Is it possible he simply overcame me with simple skill and technique? Ridiculous!?

Not giving time for him to react, Ares followed through with an attack on Archeus' stomach, causing him to fall into the violent waters.

Looking at the saber floating in the air, Ares grabbed it and was surprised at its durability and sharpness.

"To waste such a fine weapon on someone green like you. Such a waste…"

Although the weapon couldn't be called divine by quality, it was not far from it. He knew the mortal was quite resourceful, but to create a weapon close to the level of divine weapons was shocking!

"This!?"

Alas, his pondering was interrupted! Ares' face changed, and his eyes widened for a moment, recognizing something familiar to come! All of a sudden, a bolt of lightning appeared and hit him!

A hint of surprise and astonishment coursed through his body as he thought it was Zeus, but upon realizing the potency of the strike was far from usual, he turned his attention towards the still violent waves beneath.

"It is... not over..."

With a labored gasp, the man, stained with blood, gradually emerged from the water, his veins coursing with lightning.

"Heh! Finally, you are taking me seriously..." Ares muttered. The first time they clashed, he showed a glint of a smile.

Until now, the young man played according to his rules. Trying to best him in his own domain proved to be an even tougher challenge.

A foolish choice; even for the experienced gods or demigods, no known power could overcome him!

Although he was still confused, he did not remember lightning being one of Archeus' powers. Yet, out of some oddity, it seemed the youngster had access to a vast pool of powers he could draw from at any moment. If not for the boy's inexperience, rashness, and pride, there would be very few gods who could rival him.

Sadly, while his powers were good, Archeus was still too green. His actions are led by his emotions rather than his experience and vision -- something that is needed for a serious clash of gods.

His lighting compared to Zeus' is a mere tickle. Zeus would put him in his place with a simple spark if he were to challenge his domain now.

Regardless, this show of force showed some promise. A spark can grow into a raging inferno if nurtured long enough.

"Awake, mortal? Did my wake-up call manage to rouse your interest?"

Throwing the saber to Archeus, Ares reached to his side, banishing his sword to his divine armory, and called forth another weapon. A javelin, which might be too cumbersome to bear, but he easily spins it in the air.

As the God of War, he did not have many divine abilities. Among the few powers he had access to, he had a vault of weapons he could conjure up at will. And while most of them did not reach the level of the divine weapon, all of them were still powerful on their own.

"Show me what you got! Come on!"

Bellowing and taking a step, he appeared before Archeus as if he teleported, sending a countless thrust in a matter of seconds! Each attack pierced a hole in the air, making the pressure part of the water below form holes and deep craters in the muddy ground!

"So intense…!"

Archeus tried to block some of the strikes, but he realized early that it was a lost cause! He can't parry them properly due to the intensity and strength behind each attack!

As soon as one was deflected, two other strikes landed on his body, forming holes in his flesh and bones! Even pierced through his armor, which barely damped the strike before reformed due to its self-repairing property!

"What's the matter? Once again, try to beat me in my own game!? Why are you so dull!? I told you it would not work!"

Ares frowned after a mighty strike sent Archeus flying again. This mortal has improved since they started fighting. But he had little talent for this kind of combat! At this point, he is just trying to copy him in the hope he can find an opening. His moves and his style started to annoyingly resemble the clumsy version of his own.

"Come up with your own style, shitty brat."

It was not only disrespectful but even breached the boundaries of Plagiarism! Uncreative to the highest standards!

Few from my descendants would have already ended this farce after seeing such disrespect.

Not many of his bastards reached their full potency, but the few who did so almost rivaled the gods in their martial powers.

Unfortunately, as said, many even inherited his short temper and his lust for a good fight, which led them to finish fights faster than he really liked to. A quality, which he tried to suffocate and keep in line whenever he went ahead in the hope of a worthy battle.

But that's how war is usually done. Eh? Once you start to enjoy it, and once you find a really tough opponent, one of the two must fall. Battle usually only lasts a glimpse. But this glimpse is more than enough to know the other side like no other. The survivors form a hatred, or an unbreakable bond, after everything is settled.

The most beautiful aspect of war and combat was the camaraderie, which was earned through blood, sweat, and steel.

But this mortal... He has some guts. I can give him that much.

Their battle lasted for a while, and while it was evident Ares was far from going all out, he started to see him in a different light.

Other gods would already have run away or forfeited in hope that I would show mercy on them.

But Archeus? A man turned god just took his hits one after the other, and while it was easy to see he wailed in agony, he always came back for more! Yet, in war and battle, one needed more than simple toughness and berserking determination to win! One needed to think ahead and form a vision to truly become a worthy fighter and warlord!

"Foolish! Stop rushing in head first, you bollocks! Put more might behind your strikes!"

While lightning poured across the already ruined battlefield and the waters below started to evaporate and retreat from the great combat conducted above, Ares parried the strike of the saber, tanking the serenade of lightning that struck him!

His skin was visibly charred and his flesh blistered, but he ignored the attack! His pain transformed into determined might, hitting the young man in the liver and paralyzing Archeus for a few moments!

"Guehh!"

A headbutt followed, which destroyed the base of his nose, and while tears poured from his eyes, Ares grabbed the collar of his armor, throwing him far!

He is right… Why do I keep rushing against him? But even using lightning and my attacks combined, why can't I just hit him properly?

Flying a few kilometers carried by the moment, Archeus already glimpsed Ares rapidly closing! He was fast! He will be there at any moment! Even with his control over space, he just can't keep up!

"So frustrating…!"

Gritting his teeth, he pointed at Ares with his fingers, calling forth divine might in quantity and quality like never before!

He said he wanted might! He said he should stop rushing head-on! Now he will get it!

Ares stopped suddenly, feeling something immense gathering in the heavens!

Thunder started to shake the world! A whole domain of light formed and crackled through the clouds, and he just stared at them! Mesmerized by the play, the blood-red lights in his eyes, and the flames of war growing in intensity in his veins!

"That's it! That's what I am speaking about! Such passion! Such a will to overcome me! Yes... the very soul of war! Show me!"

A pillar of light formed from many individual strikes combined into one, crackling in intensity like never before! The plasma and sheer heat ignited the very air! Evaporating all the liquid below! Caving a deep hole in the place, the young god called forth everything he could muster!

"Di-Did I succeed?" Archeus heaved in slight exhaustion after what seemed like an eternal pour of power and sweat. He gave what he could spare in that attack; he only hoped it would be enough.

"I hope I wo..."

A lone figure standing in the air. Smoldering and charred mass of muscle, with crossed arms and closed eyes. Seeing that peerless physique of a statue in that state made him worry for a moment. Barely sensing a flickering divinity made it even harder to distinguish if Ares was still alive or dying.

"Suuh…" Smoke left the god's mouth as he cracked his neck, massaging it like he would wake up from a good nap. "Now that's what I am talking about. Such a feast…"

The cracked and charcoal skin fell off his body, as Ares was before Archeus before he could even recognize what really happened.

He tried to react, but it was another matter of his capability! Before he could even catch a glimpse, the towering redhead man stood before him, fully healed. Peerless, like before! No! Even more powerful!

All in all, he never experienced such a burst of speed from him! He was fast, but this was something new!

Discarding all manner of weapons, he grabbed Archeus's chestplate and forcefully made them collide with the ground. Like a true brawler, caving a deep crater in the impact.

Each strike afterwards was harder than the last! Each broke bones, tearing muscle before they could truly reform. Liquifying insides, only his ever-recovering armor kept the Archeus together!

"That's it!? That's how you want to bear the responsibility. Eh?! Boy!? That's all you got!?"

He had no choice! He thought he just wanted to ask a question, and then he was done with it! Archeus never expected he would be this close to death because of his inattention to the questioner!

With each strike, he felt he was dying, with only Eternal Vigor pulling him back to the world of the living!

No! I refuse! I refuse to die! I can't… but how can I overcome him? How?!

Archeus was cognizant of the fact that despite being a true god of Tiamat, he was weaker than the innate gods. Over time, he could remove this gap, but that takes time!

Gurgling his blood, his mind landed on the divine tree inside his mind! All the power the divine tree has, he will use. Even though it might damage his foundation, he could not fall so easily! He had to try to turn the tide, regardless of the consequences!

"Oh! I see…" His opponent grinned wildly, stopping his endless pummeling for a moment and looking up. "Now that's determination."

What followed was an apocalyptic war in the sky, like nothing seen in a long time! Even more grand than the mortal produced before! Comparable to Zeus' might for a mere moment!

"Let me taste it…" Rolling off from Archeus, Ares took a cross-legged sitting position, just watching the world rending strike, his eyes blazing up with excitement—truly the first time!

"Is he... crazy?" Archeus wondered for a moment, urging his power to teleport farther from the way of his power! Normally, he would survive, no question, but this attack? He weaved into it everything he had, even risking his godhead in the process!

In the Weave, the power he just summoned had another name: Heaven's Fall!

Yet, despite all that effort! The sacrifices he had made left him numb as he witnessed the scene before him.

An aura even more monstrous and sinister emerged from Ares, thickening and forcing its way into the world of mortals! Twisting the very reality around the God of War's imposing body!

As soon as the thick pillar of light reached a foot from Ares, it vanished without a trace! Unable to reach him or scorch his skin as he had before, the situation was even more dire than he had anticipated.

"This is unreal... how come... how come it did not hit him?!"

He was stunned, not even able to properly react, when Ares sighed and lazily walked before him.

"Eh? It is easy; I simply materialized my domain and compressed it around me. I thought you already recognized that I didn't activate it while we were fighting."

"Domain?! N-No... I thought." This was flabbergasting and humiliating! How did Archeus not recognize it? Anyway, what kind of technique was that? Was he really that weak that he was not even worthy of using such a technique against him?

"Ah! I see, so you don't know about it. Then let me explain it. You know every god has a domain? Right?"

Archeus simply nodded wordlessly; it was evident. This much, even he knew.

"Whenever we want, we can materialize our domain around us, which we can shape to serve as the amplifier of our attack or isolate and neutralize an incoming assault."

"Like a separate world?"

"Exactly! You are not that dumb, are you?" The God of War pressed his index finger against the head of the young deity, throwing the dumbstruck Archeus off balance. "Now then, if the attack does not reach sufficient strength, you will not be able to even touch the owner of the domain. Do you understand?"

Archeus lowered his head, pondering. Trying to find a way around this issue. But no matter how he rattled his brain, no solution came.

The gap is only increasing. Every time he thought he had found the true strength of the gods, something new appeared to widen the gap further. How was he supposed to remove a god's domain and close the gap?

A simple difference in divine power, ability, and technique, adding on top of this the inferiority of his domain? The result was evident. A simple issue in quality and quantity between the factions of gods! That's it! There was no easy way around it!

"I forfeit... you win." Archeus admitted that there was no way around it. Running away was also not an option. Ares would not allow that, and neither was he the kind of man to do such a cowardly act.

"Hm... I see." Ares hummed in acknowledgment, nodding as he observed the devastated "boy". "Don't fret. Losing the battle is not the end. One can win the war by losing all their battles. It is all a matter of attrition and tactics."

Like a father teaching his child, Ares removed Archus's helmet, messing up his sweaty and blood-covered hair. "You did your best, and that's what matters. You are still too weak; if we fought for real, you would not last even a strike. Learn and improve, for there is no greater teacher than failure... but also, running headstrong in a hopeless battle might prove to be your undoing one day. Choose your battles wisely. Retreating in the face of greater opposition is not always a measure of cowardice."

Archeus sighed and put his weapon away. He was frustrated at not being able to give at least a good bloody nose to the God of War. Feeling powerless and foolish standing before this mighty Adonis of man. But strangely, he was also grateful. He was different than he first expected.

Ares is definitely not just a brute... Unlike how Ares was mocked and depicted by many deities and mortals, Archues could see this firsthand.

Ares' odd and brutish ways are not because he did not put others in his eyes, but because he had the capital to fight however he wanted. After all, not many gods could rival him in a fight, despite the fact that many gods were more powerful than him.

This battle was instructive, opening his eyes to his current limits and where he needs to improve. Archeus had a long path ahead; now he had finally seen it.

Ares was right; you can win the war by losing every battle. Yet his pride dictated that he win whenever his power allowed.

And there are battles in which one can't lose, for the price is too high...

Shaking his head after nudging his numb neck, he looked at the man, who, with a raised brow and strange grin, still waited for his answer. A patient expression, which carried satisfaction.

"Ares, to your question earlier, in the world, I will create, wars will not stop but become more frequent. So there is no reason to be worried."

Ares nodded, his smile widening. "A fine, but expected answer. Even if mortals do not fight, you will definitely be fighting others. One does not become a worthy god by sitting on their laurels, but by continuously experiencing the vast world and every little battle it can offer. For every moment is a teacher of its own; remember that, young Archeus. Divinity embraces only those who covet it and do not expect it."

Archeus might not have noticed, but the gods in Olympus were surprised to hear that Ares acknowledged Archeus as a god!

He was the most vocal of the gods who did not wish to work with Archeus, a man turned god, but now he acknowledges him.

What Ares did not say was that the more divine abilities Archeus showed, the more happy he was. No god would be happy with someone who had a vast field of domains. Especially the lightning, which is the power reserved for Zeus. As for him? He just enjoyed a good battle more than anyone else, waiting for a worthy opponent since time immemorial.

Archeus showing up was a delightful surprise in his eyes. He was the first god to actually challenge him and not run away. So, to Ares, Archeus was far more worthy of the title than some of the gods watching them right now.

CHAPTER **18**

RIPPLES

(Year 257 of the Tribunal Calendar, Month of the Leo)

In Olympus, the gods were smiling after seeing Ares leave. They were on edge, and many times they wanted to interfere, but Hades and Athena stopped them. Both of them understood that if the gods interfered, it would only make things more difficult.

Ares was not the only one who hated the fact that they had to work with Archeus, and he would not be the last one.

Although Archeus did not even pose a threat, it showed the immense potential he had, which was enough to make the other gods suppress their superiority.

Athena and Hades glanced at each other and nodded.

Following behind Athena was a group of gods, including Apollo. In front of Athena, there was a golden portal, which all the gods stepped through, appearing in front of Archeus, who was waiting for them above the sea.

Looking at the group, Archeus did not say anything and simply opened a portal to Tiamat and watched them enter it.

The location of the portal that was leading to Tiamat was not close to where Maria was, so he was not worried. He even added many protections on and around the temple, just in case.

The only one who refrained from entering was Athena. She stood by Archeus' side, with a hard to read expression on her face. She had never imagined there would come a day when the gods would leave Olypmus and decide to move elsewhere.

She understood this was a foregone conclusion from the start of meeting Archeus, but it seemed everything happened so fast that it was kind of scary.

The moment she asked for a favor, Athena was aware of what she wanted, but only after talking with her uncle, Hades, did her thoughts become even more clear.

Right now, Olympus was empty, with only a few gods remaining, many of whom were in deep sleep. There is no doubt that once these gods awaken, they will decide to enter Tiamat as the only place that could become a place for them to develop.

"You have gotten what you wanted. Now that the gods are following your lead, you now need to fulfill your part of the deal."

Archeus smiled, looking at the world of Arctara. There were only two steps he would need to take before this world could truly be considered a fantasy world, but first…

"What about the Tribunal? Would they take this news well?"

Athena, without a shred of doubt in her voice, said, "They will be more than happy to see this. Although they have served us, they have always wished to become gods themselves, but since we have divided up the faith of the mortals, they could not do so."

Archeus understood this logic, as many bosses will support the growth of their subordinates to bolster their power. Only once in a while would they allow some of them to rise up, and even then, they were only bigger and more competent subordinates to use.

Even though the gods decided to enter Tiamat, it did not change the root cause of everything, nor did it increase the amount of faith in the Northern Highlands.

Right now, there are a few things he needs to do in order to fix this. One, he had to increase the overall size of the world and increase the amount of people in it. He already figured out a way to do this, which was to fuse all the planets in the solar system into Arctara, drastically increasing its size.

Archeus did not believe this was outside his capabilities since he could do this with Over Element. However, he was aware there were not just the Greek gods in this world; there were probably Norse and other gods.

The reason he had remained somewhat passive was because of these facts. While he was powerful, he couldn't contend against an entire world of gods, let alone the Chief Gods of their respective pantheons. He needed to possess his own force, which is where the Greek Gods came into the picture.

If this world was devoid of gods, he could move more freely and execute his plans in one swift motion, but caution was paramount. In the grand scheme of things, the Greek gods were not powerful.

Despite his horrible loss against Ares, this fact did not change how weak the Greek gods were.

Compared to the gods of India and the Chinese gods, the Greek gods could only be called babies. And if that was the case, he was less than an ant in front of them.

Right now, he did not place the Tribunal in his eyes, but that could not be said about the people in the Northern Highlands. If the Tribunal were left to their own devices, they could pose a threat to his plans, but from the moment the Dungeon and Mana were released, they had not made a move.

From the words of Athena, it was clear the gods have not been sending orcales to them, which means the relationship between the two has become distant.

He did not forget about the fact that they destroyed Crista and killed the villagers. He planned to make them pay for this, but for now, his actions are now to complete the basic form of a fantasy world, which he partially completed.

The dragons, dwarfs, and werewolves have added a hint of flavor to the world, but that wasn't enough.

A fantasy world had to have gods, demons, and monsters. Right now, the gods and monster parts were fulfilled, which meant he had to create the Abyss, which would be the enemy of all things, including the gods.

Creating the Abyss was easy, but creating demons was hard.

Once that was completed, the final step would be to slowly engulf the entire world, integrating them into this game.

Unknown to Archeus, the moment the gods left Olympus and entered Tiamat, many pantheons of gods around the world were confused as they no longer could sense the presence of the gods in the north.

Rome was one of the first to sense the disappearance of the gods. The One True God sent down a decree to investigate.

Egypt's divine world, led by Ra, was no different. Although they have been weaker in the past century than their counterpart Greece, the faith they got has not lessened, making them surpass the Greek divine world.

With that being said, anyone who was able to remove the Greek gods is not something they could make an enemy. If the Greek gods could disappear, they could also 'disappear'. However, even if that was the case, they still had to know what was going on.

All around the world, oracles descended from the gods, causing many factions to be on edge, feeling something was happening beneath their eyes. While not everyone received oracles, some actions could not be hidden and appeared in their eyes.

It has been many years since these ancient forces have moved, and anything they did was something for others to think about. While they did not know the inside story, it did not change the fact that the world was going to change.

Whether this change will prove beneficial or not, remains uncertain. Everything was left, hanging in the air.

(Unknown Location)

Sitting on a throne of bones, with flames flickering around, a figure seemed to look through space and time, muttering, "Which fool touched the divine pillars? Oh, it doesn't seem to have been broken, but... Eh? The monsters were released?" A hint of surprise appeared in the voice of the mysterious figure, causing some doubt.

None of the gods would release the monsters, so who could it be?

"I wonder, how long have I been asleep for? A thousand years or more? I didn't think my injuries were that serious. Well, it is fine; I do not have to worry about that bastard for a while, but I am still surprised people still worship him after so long with a response."

END OF VOLUME 1: FRAGILE WORLD OF FAITH

CHARACTER **SHEET**

Name: Almighty
Epithet: God of the beginning and the end, Most High, God
Age: ?
Race: ?
Strength: ???
Gender: ?
Role: God
Location: Earth (?)
Power: ?
Weakness: ?
Description:

Name: Apollo
Epithet: God of the Sun, God of Oracles, God of Music, God of Bards
Age: ?
Race: God
Strength: ?
Gender: Male
Role: God of the Sun, God of Olympus
Location: Tiamat
Power: ?
Weakness: ?
Description: :

Name: Archeus

Epithet: Creator of Tiamat and Archeron, First God of Tiamat, Lord of
        Death Adis, Creator of the Dark Elves, Fateless One, Foreigner,
        Jarth, Teacher, Seeker of the Truth, Abandoned Son of Earth,
        God's Chosen One

Age: 27

Race: God Race

Strength: True God of Tiamat

Gender: Male (Can assume the female gender)

Role: God of Omnipotence, Son

Location: Tiamat

Power: Eternal Vigor, Space and Time COntrol, Over Element

Weakness: None (?)

Description:

Name: Ares
Epithet: God of War, Patron Deity of Sparta, Son of the God King,
    War Maniac, Battle God of Olympus
Age: ?
Race: God
Strength: True God
Gender: Male
Role: God of Olympus
Location: Tiamat
Power: ?
Weakness: Loss of Faith
Description:

Name: Athena
Epithet: Goddess of War and Wisdom, Daughter of the God King
Age: ?
Race: God
Strength: True God
Gender: Female
Role: Goddess of Olympus
Location: Tiamat
Power: ?
Weakness: Loss of Faith
Description:

Name: August
Epithet: Devil Worshiper, True Explorer, Mad Scientist
Age: 100+
Race: Human Race (?)
Strength: ?
Gender: Male
Role: Scientist
Power: (?)
Weakness: Decaying body
Description:

Name: Dark One
Epithet: God, the Creator of Arctara, beginning and end of darkness
Age: ?
Race: God
Strength: ???
Gender: ?
Role: ?
Location: Arctara
Power: ?
Weakness: Almighty
Description:

Name: Diana
Epithet: Traumatic Survivor
Age: 26+
Race: Human Race
Strength: ?
Gender: Female
Role: Wife of the God of Dark Elves
Location: Unknown
Power: None
Weakness: Men
Description:

Name: Elima
Epithet: Traumatic Survivor
Age: 12
Race: Human Race
Strength: ?
Gender: Female
Role: Daughter of the God of Dark Elves
Location: Unknown
Power: ?
Weakness: Men
Description:

Name: Etna
Epithet: Lord of Plyos City, Saint of Poseidon, Pioneer of Magic, Disciple
    of the Archmage, Remnant of the Old Flame
Age: 35
Race: Human Race
Strength: Apprentice Mage
Gender: Male
Role: Mage
Location: Plyos City
Power: Domination Spell
Weakness: His Ambition
Description:

Name: Gyrsyra
Epithet: Dark Lord, Survivor of the Sealed Realm
Age: ?
Race: Dragon
Strength: Demigod
Gender: Male
Role: Leader of the Sealed Realm (?)
Location: Arctara
Power: ?
Weakness: ?
Description:

Name: Hades
Epithet: God of the Underworld, Brother of the God King, Enigmatic
    Ruler, God of Wealth and the Underground, Calm Observer
Age: ?
Race: God
Strength: ?
Gender: Male
Role: God of the Underworld
Location: Unknown

Power: ?
Weakness: ?
Description:

Name: Kaiser
Epithet: God of the Dark Elves, Survivor, Child of the Darkness, Devoted
    Husband and Father
Age: 26+
Race: Dark Elf
Strength: ?
Gender: Male
Role: Future God of Dark Elf, Father of a Race
Location: Unknown
Power: Shadow Walker, Dagger Mastery,
Weakness: Sunlight, Holy Magic, Lightning (?)
Description:

Name: Maria
Epithet: First Goddess of Tiamat, Outcast, Wanderer, Goddess of Magic,
    Creator of the Weave, Freedom Seeker
Age: 60+
Race: God Race
Strength: Demigod of Tiamat
Gender: Female
Role: Mother, Goddess of the God Race
Location: Tiamat's Divine Temple
Power: Weave, Temporary Spell Creation and Fate Weaver
Weakness: None
Description:

Name: Micheal
Epithet: Wrath of God, Archangel of Warriors
Age: ?
Race: Angel

Strength: ???
Gender: Male
Role: Protector of Light and Order
Location: Earth (?)
Power: ?
Weakness: ?
Description:

Name: Poseidon
Epithet: God of the Sea, Earth Shaker, Brother of the God King,
     Sovereign of Oceanic Deities
Age: ?
Race: God
Strength: ???
Gender: Male
Role: God of Olympus
Location: Unknown
Power: ?
Weakness: ?
Description:

Name: Sophia
Epithet: Brillant Mage, Daughter of Magic, Orphaned, Pioneer of Magic,
     Disciple of the Archmage
Age: 17
Race: Human Race
Strength: Apprentice Mage
Gender: Female
Role: Mage
Power: Small Healing Spell
Weakness: None (?)
Description:

Name: Teris
Epithet: Merchant of the Iron Tower, Son of Wealth, Pioneer of Magic,
    Disciple of the Archmage
Age: 24
Race: Human Race
Strength: Apprentice Mage
Gender: Male
Role: Mage, Merchant
Location: ?
Power: Fireball Spell
Weakness: His innocence
Description:

Name: Xeros
Epithet: Emperor of the World, Butcher of Men, Tyrant, Ghost King
Age: 1000+
Race: Ghost Race
Strength: Ghost King (Ancient)
Gender: Male
Role: Ruler of Archeron and the Ghost Race
Location: Archeron's Royal Palace
Power: Control over Archeron's entrances (?)
Weakness: None (?)
IDescription:

Name: Zeus
Epithet: God King of Olmpus, God of Justice and Order, God of Gods
Age: ?
Race: God
Strength: ?
Gender: Male
Role: God King of Olympus
Location: Omlympus
Power: ?

Weakness: Loss of Faith
Description:

Name: ?
Epithet: ?
Age: ?
Race: ?
Strength: ???
Gender: ?
Role: ?
Location: Unknown
Power: ?
Weakness: Poseidon
Description:

AFTERWORD

Hello readers, I am Soul River, the Author of Arch-Divinity. I figured I will tell you a little bit about myself and how this came to be.

I started writing when I was around 12 years old. Around this time, I have just left Jamaica and found myself in a foreign country, in the form of the United States of America. It was difficult for me to make friends as I felt there was a cultural barrier. No matter what I did, even if it was a simple joke, I would have to repeat it, so others could understand. I rarely spoke to people because of that and fell in love with reading. To this day, I am still at loss as to why I picked up a laptop and began writing. English was not my favorite subject, Mathematics was. To me, numbers were like a new language that no matter where you are from, everyone could understand.

That day, looking at the blank screen, I saw a world of infinite possibilities. The only thing that could limit me, was my imagination. I started by writing fanfiction of Overlord and Naruto, slowly discovering my own writing style and began to write my original stories. In the beginning, my writing was not good but over the years, it has gotten much better.

I am more of a descriptive writer than anything else. I like to describe a scene and let the readers imagine it inside their minds. I want them to be able to feel and sense the scene I want to depict.

Arch - Divinity is one of the many stories I have in my vault of stories but was the one closest to being finished. It might be crazy to say this but, I do not think this is even in the top ten works I have. The style of writing, descriptive storytelling, have suffered greatly here. If not because of the above reason, I do not think I would release this story. After all, it was a project that evolved into a story of its own.

There are many things that went unanswered, which I know you want the answer to. In the following books, they will be answered. I hope you are satisfied with the answer you will receive.

I still have much room to grow and I would like to go through this process with people who can appreciate and understand the difficulties of putting one's thoughts on a paper. Hopefully, in the following books, I can showcase my growth to you, my loyal audience. I do not have a timeline for it yet, but eventually it will be out.

Editors: Anima Libera (Grammar Editor), Chyenne Lyons (Grammar
    Editor),
Illustrators: O.u.rs_creation (Athens Illustration)

The two leaves blows in the wind,
always so close but never to touch.
The light of the moon cast a shadow over man,
but the sun was all he saw.
Soul River | 2024

www.ingramcontent.com/pod-product-compliance
Lightning Source LLC
Chambersburg PA
CBHW030926260626
47169CB00002B/387